THE

THE ATTIC

THE BOX IN
THE ATTIC

BY

NAN TURNER

www.bookstandpublishing.com

Published by
Bookstand Publishing
Morgan Hill, CA 95037
3708_4

ISBN 978-1-61863-341-5

Printed in the United States of America

DEDICATION

LILY'S STORY was dedicated to the over 1.2 million persons in the United States and Canada who suffer from Parkinson's Disease. I would like to dedicate *THE BOX IN THE ATTIC* to all those researchers who are working to find a cure for this devastating neurological disease.

As in any research funding is usually in short supply. I will donate 10% of my personal sales and my royalties from the "Lily" books to Parkinson's Disease research.

NAN TURNER/DARLENE EICHLER
JULY, 2012

ACKNOWLEDGEMENTS

Words of thanks and appreciation go to my husband, George, who has helped in many ways to get this book out to my readers. He brought in dinner, ran errands, (especially emergency runs to get ink cartridges), proof read, assisted in editing and revisions. I couldn't have done it without you.

And to my readers...without your encouragement I couldn't have done it. You gave me the strength to keep going when I felt like stopping.

Nan Turner/Darlene Eichler
July, 2012

SUMMARY OF "THE ROSE SERIES"

THE JOURNEY HOME: In this first book of "The Rose Series," Rose Collins is a twelve year old Melungeon girl from the mountains of Kentucky, recently orphaned. She is sent to live with her only relative, Aunt Margaret, who lives and works on the Keller Estate in Virginia. This is the early 1950s and Rose encounters bigotry in school, primarily by Carl Cutlipp. After an accident Rose's blood is typed revealing that she has been adopted. The hunt for her birth parents takes them back to Kentucky and an orphanage that keeps showing up in rose's dreams. Upon their return they discover that Mr. Keller has died; there begins the twist and turns of finding the rightful heir of the Keller fortune. Will it be Aunt Margaret or William Keller, an unknown half-brother who seems to appear from nowhere? (Lily, whose Mother works for the Kellers and the Estate becomes Rose's close friend) The answer can be found in the second book, "View From the Attic."

VIEW FROM THE ATTIC, the second book in "The Rose Series," picks up the struggle to determine who is the rightful heir to the Keller Estate.

In the meantime Rose continues to encounter the prejudice of race through the spokesman of her classmate, Carl Cutlipp, Rose deals with Carl's illness, another trip to Bridgetown which brings sadness and adventure. Aunt Margaret and James are married in a spring ceremony. A strange woman, dressed in a blue suit shows up and she turns out to be Rose's "Granny Esther." The newlyweds leave on their honeymoon to the Great Smoky Mountains with Rose in tow. Their effort to keep her from Esther turns out to be a comedy of errors with a cast of mountain characters. The remainder of the story recounts the finality of the rightful heir story and the move to the Keller Mansion. Rose and Lily have seemed to grow closer, Lily spending the night often in the little attic room. But after the big birthday party Lily has withdrawn from Rose, joining the clique of girls at school who made fun of Rose. The adults and Rose were puzzled and disappointed at this turn of events.

PROMISES TO KEEP, the third book in "The Rose Series," follows Rose through her senior year in high school. The book recounts the end of the rightful heir story and the move to the Keller Mansion. The inheritance does not ensure Rose and her family, or friends, that life will be without its stresses and crises. There is a tragic fire, an attack on Margaret, an intricate web of lies to hurt Rose at school and a near fatal traffic accident.

Granny Esther becomes an important factor in Rose's life along with an eclectic cast of characters, some new and others who become more involved in the lives of Rose, Margaret, and James.

RETURN TO BRIDGETOWN, the fourth book in "The Rose Series," begins the summer after Rose's graduation from high school. Her friend, Lily, marries against everyone's advice. A new house takes shape on the site of the Keller Mansion, which burned to the ground in "View From the Attic."

Rose enters college and meets her first love, Lewis David, who turns out not to be the person he claims to be. The summer finds her nursing her Granny Esther back to good health. She begins to rethink her major in college. She receives a speeding ticket from a handsome red-haired policeman. This may be the beginning of a long lasting romance for Rose.

ROSE'S SONG, the fifth and final book in "The Rose Series," finds Rose in Nursing School in Kentucky near her Granny Esther. Her friends and family endure joys and tragedies as this series comes to an end.

CHARACTER LIST FOR *THE BOX IN THE ATTIC*

LILY FAIN LAWSON — April 15, 1940. To Anna and Frank Fain. She becomes Rose's best friend in the "Rose Series." She elopes with Douglas Lawson and they have Anna Rose. The marriage ends in divorce.

DOUGLAS LAWSON — Married to Lily when very young, father of Anna Rose. He shows maturity and tries to get Lily to notice him again. He is an attentive and good father to Anna Rose.

ANNA ROSE LAWSON — Born August 18, 1960 (daughter of Lily and Doug-named for Lily's mother Anna and Rose. Dark hair and blue eyes. A happy baby.

Anna Fain Litton — Lily's mother born in Rose Hill, Va.. Divorced from first husband, Lily's father. Married Abe Litton when Lily was a teenager. Warm, outgoing, did domestic work for the Kellers and Margaret and James. Died after Lily was married. Buried in Church cemetery.

Rose Collins McCray — Main character in the *Rose Series*. She appears in the "Lily Books" as Lily's friend and confidant. She brings back memories of the little house overlooking the Keller Estate.

Aunt Margaret Collins Keller Robinson — The matriarch of the *Rose Series*. She became Rose's unofficial mother when Rose was orphaned at age twelve. She worked for the wealthy Keller family and at one time was married to John Keller. She and James are happily married and live in a new house, Bittersweet, built after the original mansion burned.

James Robinson — Aunt Margaret's faithful and loving husband. He was the former butler and manager of the

Keller Mansion. He has taken the place of Rose's father over the years.

Abe Litton — Formerly married to Lily's mother, Anna. After her death he married Sarah. He is a good father to Lily and grandfather to Anna Rose. He has suffered from Parkinson's Disease for several years.

Sarah Litton — A professional nanny and married to Abe. She is a kind and caring person and is of great help and a surrogate mother to Lily.

Teresa Fain (nee Taylor) — Everyone believes is a sincere young lady, except Lily. She is out to get Lily, her half sister. She insists that she deserves all of her father's inheritance because he loved Lily more than she.

Jimbo — Young lad of questionable age who aids Teresa in finding John Mason in Masonberg.

Andy McCray — Rose's husband who works in Law Enforcement.

James Andrew McCray — Newborn son of Rose and Andy McCray.

CHAPTER ONE

A sliver of light struggled to break through the hazy attic window. Teresa waited for her eyes to adjust to the dimness and then began her search. Her father's Will had to be here somewhere.

She hadn't noticed the rusty metal box hiding in the shadows on her previous trip. Slipping her hand into the box, its cool metal giving her a start, she felt for its contents. Immediately her pulse quickened as she retrieved the packet of papers, carefully tied with a yellowing cord. Placing the letters under her shirt, she began her descent down the rickety ladder. Trembling with excitement as a child on Christmas morning, Lily must have given her thoughts over to an exciting adventure-the means to buy whatever her heart desired-a fancy car, a new home, or money to travel around the world. The possibilities were endless. Several minutes went by before she could untie the old cord which had begun to disintegrate in the heat of several summers. Gently she unfolded the sheets one by one, placing them in a single layer on the dining room table, trying at the same time to read the words at the top of each page. Not one said "Final Will and Testament" as she was hoping but it turned out to be a handwritten letter. She recognized her Father's large, flowing handwriting immediately.

Dear Teresa,
I hope you found this letter in your search for the Will. The Will won't be found until you

accomplish everything listed below. Please don't think I'm being cruel. I feel you need to learn the lessons put forth in my requests which have been given much thought. I have been concerned about your attitude toward others, particularly Lily.

1.   Find your half-sister, Lily, and do something good for her without her knowing you did it. Write this on a piece of paper, send it to the address at the bottom of this page.

2.   If your Mother is still living, write her a letter and tell her how much she has meant to you. Send a copy to the address at the end of this letter.

3.   Choose a church and go every Sunday for a month. Send your attendance record to the address at the end of this letter.

4.   Ask Lily and her family to go out for a meal with you. Send the receipt to the address at the end of this letter.

5.   Find a family in need and give them a basket of food. Send the receipt and a description to the address at the end of this letter.

6.   Write a 1000 word essay on why you think I asked you to do these things. Be honest. Send it to the address below with a recent photo.

Teresa, I love you and want you to be a loving sister to Lily. If you have met all these requirements you will receive instructions on how to locate the Will.

Love, Dad
Send to:
Mr. John Mason
P.O. Box 155
Masonberg, Virginia

She didn't know whether to laugh or cry. She hadn't realized her Father was such a conniver, determined to have two daughters who acted just like Lily, the favorite one. The more she thought about the letter the madder she became. Why did he think she wanted to be like Lily in order to find the Will? Now that she had met Lily she thought her rather dull and mousey.

Teresa had to find a way out of this.....maybe she could make a trip to Masonberg. She wasn't quite sure where it was but she would find out. Tomorrow was Saturday and she would make it her mission to find the obscure town and go there if it wasn't too far away.

It was a sunny, warm autumn day in the Bristol, Virginia area. Teresa was in deep thought and missed the changing colors of the hardwood trees. The shadows were growing longer, a barometer of cooler weather. Teresa stopped at the last service station before making the turn onto Route 11. An elderly man slowly walked to the driver's side of the car.

"Fill 'er up miss?" He liked to call his customers by name but he couldn't place this girl. Must be one of them new ones in that fancy housing unit up the road a piece.

"No thank you, I have enough gas. I need some information." He opened his mouth to speak but she kept on. "Can you tell me where Masonberg is located? I hope it's not far."

"Well, Ma'am since you don't need gas you must have near on to a tankful. Masonberg is a good piece from here, maybe about a hundred mile."

Teresa didn't show any response. "In which direction? I really need to go today."

"It's northeast of here. The road gets a little crooked and narrow. If you have plenty of time you should be okay. Wouldn't you feel better if you had a little more gas in this old car? Sorry, I didn't mean to criticize, but she does have some age on her."

"Yes, yes, she does. I don't have a lot of money. Put in maybe two gallons. That should do it."

There was something about the girl that touched him. He put in three gallons instead of two and charged her for the amount she requested.

He drew a crude map on the back of a dirty receipt retrieved from the ground. She thanked him and began the hundred mile adventure. The day was just right for traveling. And a perfect time to reflect on her situation and her Father's strange letter. She wondered if her Mother would have agreed with him. She didn't think so because she got the impression that Lily wasn't one of her favorite people either.

As Teresa sped along she was trying to come up with a plan to locate Mr. John Mason. She had in her mind that Masonberg was very small and everyone should know all the residents. But what if they didn't? She began to think that she needed more information before she went on this trip which might turn out to be a wild goose chase..

Although she came across as having a tough exterior she was basically a shy person. Strangers made her uncomfortable. She made her decision.......she would do this another day.

Teresa made a U-turn on the desolate country road.

*****

Lily searched for a tissue in the glove box. She knew the tears were coming. Starting the car she was thinking how good things never seem to stay the same. She wondered if Miss Rosalytta was still living. Maybe she died and there was no one to care for the little yellow house and it just fell down. It died from lack of love and attention. She could only guess but she was deeply saddened not to find Miss Rosalytta or the yellow house. Lily dabbed at the tears trickling down her checks.

It was past her naptime and Anna Rose was restless. Lily needed to hurry home and stop obsessing on the past. Today was important, she knew nothing about tomorrow but she wished she could see into the future.

She turned on the radio, hoping the music would put Anna Rose to sleep. As she drove back toward Bristol her mind wandered to the years when she and Rose were in high school. She looked forward to spending the night in the little attic room overlooking the big Keller Estate. Although she and Rose were the best of friends she had envied her dark beauty and outgoing personality since the day they met. She had tried to emulate her in so many ways when they were younger. Now she envied her happiness and love of a great husband. Maybe someday she would have all of that if she chose the right man to marry.

She suspected Rose didn't understand the problem she had with three men vying for her attention. That's no surprise. Lily didn't understand it either. One time Rose even laughed when Lily told her she got the dates mixed up and thought a different person was coming to the door. Lily knew this situation couldn't go on forever. She would make her choice soon even though Madame Rosalytta was not there to give advice. Her Mother would probably say that God had a hand in her not finding the fortuneteller today. Maybe she was right.

Lily was almost home when she noticed some of the leaves had begun to turn. Fall was her favorite time of year. The welcome crispness in the air seemed always to give her an extra boost of energy. Perhaps she would suggest to Tom that they go for a ride and a picnic on the Blue Ridge Parkway this week-end. He was more likely to go since he was the outdoor type. She admired him for that quality having been a tomboy growing up in the rolling foothills of those beautiful mountains..

If she asked David, the doctor, to go he would say that right now his weekends were taken up with working. He would probably suggest they have a quiet supper at home and watch television. If she asked Doug he would want to spend the week-end which meant staying overnight and she would not do that. She thought he felt it was okay to stay together since they were once married and she tried to explain why she felt it was wrong. Talking to Rose about her feelings might have helped but time with her best friend was rare.

As she pulled into a space in front of her apartment building she noticed Sarah's car parked down the street. She couldn't tell if anyone was in it. She carefully lifted the sleeping Anna Rose and carried her to the entrance. Sarah was standing there at the top of the steps. She held the door for the young mother and her sleeping child.

"Thanks, Sarah. To what do I ....and then she noticed her face. Sarah, what's wrong? Is it Abe?"

"No, sweetheart it isn't Abe. It's Tom."

"Tom! What has happened? Has he been in an accident?"

"I'm sorry to say, yes. He had stopped to see if someone was in a burning house."

"But Tom is not a fireman! Where was this, Sarah? You're frightening me. Tell me the truth." She grabbed Sarah's arm in her efforts to get her to say what she wanted to hear.

"Listen to me, Lily. He thought someone was in the old Cutlipp house on Red Barn Road. Some transients had been sleeping there recently. Mr. Cutlipp passed away about three years ago in a nursing home and no one had lived there permanently for years."

She saw Lily's face turn ghostly white and she knew she understood what was coming next. "I'm sorry, Lily, but the roof caved in and Tom didn't make it out". She started to go down and Sarah grabbed Anna Rose. She knelt, holding the baby securely, and began to gently shake Lily.

"Lily, do you hear me?" She sat the baby on the ground and started to pat Lily's face as the distraught young woman began turning her head from side to side. Reaching over she touched Anna Rose and her baby smiled at her Mother. Then the rush of tears began. There was no controlling the sobs that wracked her body.

Sarah helped Lily to her feet and picked up the baby and with gentle guidance assisted them into the building and up the stairs to their apartment. Sarah placed the baby in her play pen and guided Lily to the end of the sofa, the housewarming gift from her and Abe. There on the end table, smiling from its frame, was a picture of Tom in his uniform.

"Sarah, please tell me it's a mistake. He is such a good person. This couldn't happen to him. He took the job because he wanted to help people. He talked often of how he wanted to be a doctor but couldn't afford to go to medical school." The tears started to flow again. Anna Rose looked at her Mother and began to cry softly.

Sarah was at a loss as to what to say to ease Lily's pain. A few days ago she told Abe she thought Lily would choose Tom as her husband. He had agreed but said how much he felt for all four of the young people. They were so kind and good and he knew there would be two persons who would suffer a great loss.

"Lily, I don't know how much you are hurting but I do know it must be extremely painful. Tom had become very special to you after he spent time in the hospital. It was a beautiful love story....you two getting together several years after graduating high school." She reached over and squeezed the grieving woman's hand.

The door bell rang, startling Lily. Sarah hurried to answer it. Opening the door just a little, Sarah saw Doug standing there with tears streaming down his cheeks. Lily ran toward him and she fell into his open arms. He knew about Tom. She felt a comforting sense of warmth in his arms.

"I'm so sorry, Lily. I know how much he meant to you. Tom was such a decent person. I had been thinking that you would be telling me soon that you two were engaged. It would be difficult for me to say you made a bad choice.

I find it hard to admit this but I think you two belonged together."

Lily couldn't believe her ears. He had finally grown up. How sad it took a divorce to help him mature into a responsible adult. She stood back and looked him in the eye. Even his countenance had changed. She wondered if there had been a special person in his life who encouraged him.

"Lily, is there anything I can do to help you at this time? Anything?" He removed his handkerchief and wiped the tears from his eyes. She started to say no but then she thought of Anna Rose. She loved her daddy and it would be a special time if they could be together now.

"Doug, would you keep Anna Rose while I visit with Tom's Mother? I have no idea what will be expected of me."

She took his hand and led him to the sofa and sat down. He saw the sadness and weariness in her eyes. How would she get through this tragedy? It seemed her life had been one problem and crisis after another lately. Tom had been her rock, her confidant. That was all gone. She wished Rose had more time for their friendship but her life was filled with her family.

"Lily, I'll be glad to keep her for a few days. I had planned to take some time off anyway. Do you feel like helping me get some of her things together?"

"Of course. Would you get the small suitcase out of the hall closet?"

Sarah watched this scene playing out in front of her. She had always liked Doug and felt sorry for him.

"Lily, if you'll hold Anna Rose I'll help Doug get her clothes. I think that's a fine idea for daddy and daughter to spend time together. I'll have her things ready in a few minutes."

Lily sat down, took Tom's picture off the table and hugged it to her chest. The tears started again.

Doug came back into the room, a suitcase in one hand and Anna Rose secure in his other arm. She was asleep and her head rested on his shoulder. Lily took in the touching scene and put it away for another time. She could only think of Tom at this moment.

"I'll call when I get her home and tucked into bed. I don't think she'll know that she isn't here."

"She has had a long day and I know she feels the sadness. She doesn't see her Mother cry that often. Thank you, Doug. I can barely deal with me tonight and you know how our little girl loves to be with her Daddy."

Lily could tell by the droop of his shoulders he was sad, too.

"I'll call you soon, Lily."

"Good night, Doug." She closed the door softly.

CHAPTER TWO

Teresa found it impossible to fall asleep. She reread the letter from her father several times and still found it unbelievable that he would put such a task on her. What did she care about Lily and her family? They would never accept her. She knew that deep in her soul. What was he thinking? She heard the mantle clock strike twelve and then one. Making her way to the kitchen, she took the milk container from the refrigerator. Its lightness reminded her she had forgotten to buy groceries. Giving the carton a sniff, she poured the dribble of sour milk down the drain.

As she passed the old desk, a family relic for over a hundred years, she felt a strange pull toward it. Her father's letter from the attic box was there in plain view. Why did she feel compelled to read it again? Nothing would have changed. What was this feeling? Could it have been a sense of dread for all the things her father wanted her to do, or maybe it was the deep loneliness she felt as she thought of the premature deaths of her parents? She had no one...not a soul ... no one who cared if she lived or died. She knew she came across as tough but she found that image harder to maintain with each passing day.

Taking out the letter, she began to read it for at least the tenth time. "Number one, find your half sister, Lily, and do something for her without her knowing it" Now what would she do for Lily? She knew where she lived, so that wasn't a problem. What could she do? She could think of several things but her father wouldn't approve. If she had to she would do it tomorrow and get it over with. But what?

Maybe it would come to her if she made her way to Bristol. She could always say she came to see the baby. She had to admit she was a cute one.

*****

Lily didn't sleep well. It was a long night and she wished she could have gotten up and gone to the funeral home. She was thankful Doug took the baby home with him. She needed to say good-bye to Tom alone. Knowing that would not be the proper thing to do, she would go with Abe and Sarah sometime this morning. She wondered if Tom's Mother would want her to be there. After all they weren't married, not even engaged. She had never been certain if his Mother cared for her. She leaned toward the negative. Maybe today she would know for sure.

Teresa was getting up about the same time as Lily. Knowing it was too early to visit anyone Teresa made herself a pot of coffee and went next door to "borrow" her neighbor's morning paper. Mrs. Flynn didn't get up until after ten and she would never know that Teresa had read her Daily Herald.

Making herself comfortable in her Dad's old recliner, she opened the paper and began to read the headlines. One, in particular caught her eye, "Fireman killed trying to save homeless man." She quickly scanned the article and something made her go back and read the fireman's name again. Thomas A. Williams. The name was familiar. Then she remembered…. the young man Lily had been dating. Oh, poor Lily! I shouldn't feel so bad for her, but to lose someone you love is not good. There must be something I can do and Lily won't have to find out. There will be people around showing concern and sympathy. This is going to be easier than I thought.

*****

Sarah and Abe, unable to sleep, talked until they heard the clock strike midnight. Lily had mentioned to Sarah that she wanted to go to the funeral home early in the morning. This troubled Sarah. She knew Lily had not been close to Patsy Williams.

"Abe, what do you think about Lily going?" Abe heard the doubt in her soft voice. He understood why Lily wanted to be there but he didn't want to see her hurt by someone's unkind words.

"I have my doubts, but Sarah, Lily is an adult and she needs to do what she feels is right for her."

"I know you're right, like you usually are, my dear."

Soon they had drifted off to sleep, both agreeing they must trust Lily to do the right thing.

*****

The phone rang early that morning......the first day after Tom's death. The person calling was about to hang up when a man's voice said, "hello." Patsy Williams thought she had the wrong number.

"Who's calling, please?" She was glad he asked the question.

"This is Patsy Williams, Tom's Mother. Is Lily able to come to the phone?" Abe heard the sadness in her voice.

"I'll see if she is awake. I know she would like to talk to you. Just a minute."

"Hello, Mrs. Williams. How are you this morning?" She really didn't know what else to say.

"I'm probably no better than you are, Lily. Will you come over to my house today? There are some things I need to ask you and some things I know Tom would like for me to say to you." Lily could hear her sobbing.

I'll be right over as soon as I can." She would skip breakfast.

Sarah was up and in the kitchen making coffee. Her night had been restless but she would try to put that aside to be of help to Lily and Abe.

She and Abe were talking quietly when Lily came in.

"Mrs. Williams wants me to come over there. I'll get dressed and go in a few minutes."

"Lily, I'll drive you and I'll just stay in the car."

"Abe, I know you don't feel well early in the morning and I'll be okay to drive myself over. You and Sarah stay here and have a good breakfast. There are eggs and bacon in the refrigerator. I don't know if she will ask me to go to the funeral home but I'll go if she does."

"Lily, you do whatever you feel the need to do. We'll stay here just in case someone calls or comes to see you."

"I don't know what I would do without you two and Anna Rose is always asking where is Abie and Grammy Sarah."

"She is a bright spot in our lives. We know you have a stressful job and we're there whenever you need us."

14

"Thank you." Giving him a kiss on his forehead, she hesitated as if she wanted to say more. But instead, turned and hurried to her room.

Only once had Lily been to Tom's home since they had been dating. It was the one subject they left alone since that one time he took her to meet his Mother. Lily thought of it many times and had even talked to Rose about why it turned out the way it did. The only thing she could come up with was that Patsy Williams had been terribly hurt by Tom's father. George Williams had not been a good father or husband, leaving a young wife to raise Tom alone. He was killed in a drunken brawl when Tom was about four years old. The shame of it and the lack of income no doubt had affected Patsy William's self esteem. She was overly protective of Tom and felt threatened by anyone who came into his life.

Lily turned on to Linden Street unsure of which house belonged to Mrs. Williams. Going at a snail's pace, she spotted Tom's truck parked in the driveway. A feeling of deep despair swept over her as she thought about how he would never enjoy his pride and joy again. He had worked extra jobs to help buy the shiny black truck.

She pulled into the driveway behind the truck. Sitting there for a few seconds she thought about what she might say to Mrs. Williams. It would be difficult but she would remember they both had loved Tom and were hurting more than words could express.

Knocking on the door, Lily waited for a response but not a sound came from within the house. She knocked louder this time and heard footsteps. A woman opened the door and asked her to come in. Her eyes were red and puffy, obviously from crying but this couldn't be Patsy Williams. This woman had snow white hair and lines at the corner of her eyes. She moved as if she were quite old.

"Lily, won't you come in the kitchen and have some breakfast? I know you didn't have time to eat before you left home." She led the way into a room filled with light. Although the kitchen was small it was cheery and inviting. Mrs. Williams gestured toward a chair at a small table with an arrangement of yellow flowers in the center.

"Do you drink coffee, Lily?" She had a coffee pot in her hand ready to pour the steaming liquid into her cup.

"I couldn't do without it. Yes, thank you. I don't know any nurses at the hospital who don't drink coffee."

Mrs. Williams brought a plate from the oven and set it in front of Lily. The aroma of eggs and bacon were pleasant to her. She had not felt hungry until now. Perhaps it was because she was sitting at the table where Tom ate every day.

"Lily, we've talked very little in the past eighteen months you have been seeing my son. I'll admit I didn't agree with him seeing a divorced woman with another man's child. I guess I'm old fashioned that way. Just in the past month I had started to change my attitude toward you. I don't believe Tom told you but I am dying of stomach cancer. I saw the expression on your face when I opened the door. I want to say how very sorry I am that you and Tom won't have a life together. You made a handsome couple. He loved you with all his heart and Anna Rose, too."

She got up from the table and went to the counter, opened a bottle of pills and swallowed two. The nurse in Lily wanted to ask what they were but she did not.

"Mrs. Williams, I can't tell you how sorry I am that you lost your only child. Tom and I had a special relationship. As you probably know there are two other men in my life but I think I was about to tell Tom I wanted to spend the rest of my life with him." Lily broke down and began to sob. The grieving woman came over and put her arm around Lily's shoulders.

She stood up and wrapped her arms around the emaciated woman. They stood in the sunny kitchen and cried; one for a son and one for a lover.

CHAPTER THREE

Do people ever get used to going to funerals? It seemed that some older folk, especially women, took pleasure in going. Lily remembered how they used to put their heads together before the service. She guessed they were comparing this service to the last one they attended. Lily felt uncomfortable and out of place…she would rather be anywhere today than here sitting on the front pew with Tom's Mother. The red carnations had an annoying aroma but Lily couldn't remember why they bothered her.

Patsy Williams was a young mother. She was only sixteen when she ran away and married Tom's father. Lily didn't have the nerve to ask why she never remarried after her divorce. Maybe she was afraid she would marry someone like George H. Williams. Lily wouldn't have known his name except it was right here in this little funeral paper. Tom was young, just a few months older than Lily and his whole life was condensed into this folded piece of paper from Baxter's Funeral Service. His date of birth, the dash that represented the few short years he had lived, and then his death, survived by his mother Patsy Young Williams. He was predeceased by his father, George H. Williams. No mention of the love of his life, Lily Fain Lawson. Mr. Williams (Tom would laugh at Mr.) was employed by the Washington County Emergency Medical Crew. Services will be held on Monday at River Bend Baptist Church at 2:00 P.M. Burial following in the church cemetery.

The red carnations! They were the flowers on her Mother's casket. She hoped the service would be short and she wouldn't throw up. The color had drained from her face. She felt dizzy.

The remainder of the service was a blur to Lily. She recalls Patsy reaching over and patting her hand. The music started and six young men dressed in EMT uniforms walked up to the front of the church. Two funeral home employees rolled the casket down the aisle toward the door as the six young men followed.

The next thing she remembered was seeing the six men place the casket over a large hole in the ground. That was it. Then she recalls she is in Abe's car headed for her apartment. She kept thinking that she didn't want to end this chapter of her life.

*****

Sarah and Abe were always there for Lily, no matter the time or place. Many evenings had been spent discussing which of her three suitors would make the best husband and father. Sometimes they agreed and others they would have chosen differently. But they both agreed that Lily's love for Tom was the kind for which love stories were created. Thomas Williams was a romantic at heart. Arrangements of flowers would appear on rainy Mondays and Lily never knew when her favorite chocolate candy would magically appear on her desk at work. He expressed his love to Lily and Anna Rose in so many little ways. Lily's friends, particularly Rose, didn't understand why Lily had a problem choosing among the three suitors. In their eyes Tom won hands down.

*****

Teresa enjoyed shopping for groceries. She had always tagged along with her father on his weekly trips to the grocery store. She looked forward to the smells and the many varieties of products found on the shelves. As a very small child her father kept saying not to touch but she was too fascinated to keep her hands off the foods of interesting shapes and colors.

These trips served her well as an adult and she prided herself on being a frugal shopper. It occurred to her that Lily might have extra people coming to her house. They would need to be fed. It would be easy to leave a basket of groceries at Lily's door and no one would be the wiser. She would have to date the receipt and send it to that person who lived in Masonberg, wherever that was. She would take the time to go there very soon.

Teresa spent all the money she had for Lily's groceries. Realizing that her monthly stipend set up by her father wouldn't come for another week, she took a few of the groceries out of the bags for herself. She had kept the bill under a decent amount until she remembered Anna Rose. She didn't know what the little girl liked or what she was allowed to have. Then, it was as if she heard her father's voice talking about how healthy Lily's Mother fed her. Maybe she would not allow the baby to have sweets. She was making too much of a simple gesture to fulfill her father's wishes. If they didn't want what she bought, so what? She had done an act of kindness and she hoped no one found out.

The store was busy today. She had hoped to finish sooner so there wouldn't be a chance of being seen by Lily or anyone in her family. Teresa took a chance on double parking as she hurried into Lily's apartment building. She gently placed the two large bags of groceries in front of apartment seven. She wondered if she had remembered the number correctly. Then she thought...who would know if the wrong person received the food? She had met her obligation.

She heard a key turn in a lock. Oh God, don't let it be Lily. Looking up she saw that it was the door next to Lily's apartment. An elderly lady stepped out and slowly turned in Teresa's direction.

"What's going on there young lady? Why don't you ring the bell? Someone is there while poor Lily attends her boy friend's funeral. Such a sad thing to happen."

Teresa hurried away without a word.

*****

Lily couldn't stop the music in her head. 'Amazing grace how sweet the sound that saved a wretch like me.' she had been such a fool. Maybe if she had chosen Tom to be her husband he wouldn't have been going down Red Barn Road that fatal night. 'I once was lost, but now I'm found.' No, I don't see why Tom was taken away from me. Please make the music stop. She began to cry, softly at first and then the sobs came strong and uncontrollable. She had been such a foolish woman. And now she and Anna Rose would pay the price over and over.

She had persuaded Sarah and Abe to go home. Abe looked exhausted. Lily wondered if he had taken all his medication. She and Sarah had noticed how forgetful he had become lately.

CHAPTER FOUR

Lily fought going to sleep. She wanted to remember everything about Tom, the way he looked, his smell, his soft, soothing voice. She was afraid sleep and nightmares would begin to erase memories of him. She had heard patients say that they had difficulty in remembering their loved ones' faces. She couldn't imagine not remembering Tom, not that beautiful face; those eyes that seemed to penetrate one's deepest thoughts. He would be etched in her memory forever. She had no doubt.

Lily must be dreaming. She thought she heard sounds coming from the kitchen. The aroma of fresh perked coffee made its way into the room. Only one person in her life would be in her kitchen in the middle of the night. David! It would be like him to come and check on her and make coffee before he left.

A pang of guilt shot though Lily. Tom was dead for less than a week and she was thinking warm thoughts about David, hoping he was in the kitchen. Throwing on her robe, she hurried down the hall and pushed open the kitchen door. She was wrong. It wasn't David. Doug stood there with a sleeping Anna Rose in his arms.

"It's hard to make coffee with a baby in your arms," he whispered. His smile was a comforting sight for Lily on this restless night.

"Give her to me. What are you doing here so early or should I say so late?" Lily felt a warmth go through her tired body. No, I won't, I won't give in she kept saying over and over to herself.

"Lily, I know I should have called but I was afraid you were asleep. I can only imagine how you are feeling tonight. I know how I would feel if something happened to you." There were tears in his eyes.

"Please Doug, let's not talk about such sad things. I'll put the baby to bed and then we'll talk while we have coffee."

It was all he could do to keep from taking Lily in his arms and apologize for the trouble he had caused her in the past. He loved her dearly and would do whatever he could to get her back. But he felt that Lily looked at him only as a friend and Anna Rose's father. He would not mess that up.

*****

Teresa felt safe in her Father's old recliner. She could almost feel his arms around her. The worn brown chair no longer had the scent of his spicy aftershave but had taken on the odors of the mold which seemed intent on creeping into the drafty house. Sometimes late at night she imagined the mold as a black monster with tentacles like an octopus. It crawled from the hall closet down the hall and then it began to creep slowly up the stairs, one at a time. It seemed to hesitate at the top of the stairs and she heard it sliding along the floor headed straight for her room. It slithered slowly as a slimy snail might do. Then she heard it slide under the door. Closer to her bed. Closer and then suddenly she awoke, for it was a dream she had almost every night.

*****

Teresa took the crumpled sheet of paper from her pocket. She felt anger at her father every time she had to check something off the list. Why would he expect her to be friendly with Lily? They would never be close. She didn't think a bag of groceries and some lip service to Lily would change a lot. Why couldn't she make her own list? It would have things on it like start a rumor about Lily. One that would hurt her relationship with her doctor boy friend. Or one that would turn Doug against her. She didn't understand why he wanted her back. He should be glad she left him.

I wonder why she did leave him. Somehow I must find out. My chance will come. And then she began to plan how she could find out more about Lily Lawson and her failed marriage.

*****

The ringing of the telephone awakened Margaret. James had taken something for his headache and gone to bed early. As she reached across him she knew he didn't hear the ring.

"Hello. This is Margaret Robinson." Her hand shook.

"Aunt Margaret, I think I'm losing the baby." Her voice was so dim that Margaret almost said, "You have the wrong number."

"Rose, is that you, honey? What's wrong?" She hoped she hadn't heard right.

"Aunt Margaret, Andy is away taking a class and I'm cramping and bleeding. Tell me what to do." Margaret had not heard that from Rose since she was in high school and dealing with Carl Cutlipp.

"Rose, hang up and call an ambulance. Then call Andy. He should be with you. I'll hang up now and you call for help." She heard the receiver click.

"What's wrong, Margaret?" Is it Rose or the baby?" James was awake now.

"Yes, and she thinks she is losing the baby. It's too early and Andy is out of town. I wish she lived closer. James, what can we do?"

"I don't think either one of us is able to get in the car and go to Johnston City tonight. Do you?"

"No, I agree. Let's wait and see what morning brings. Rose was so frightened even though she is a nurse. She probably knows more than she told me."

"Now, Margaret, let's don't borrow things to worry about. I'll go and make some hot chocolate. How does that sound?"

"I'll be right down. There won't be any sleep for me tonight." She knew James would be sitting up with her.

The ambulance came fast. Rose knew the driver and when he heard her name he lost no time in reaching her house.

The doctor and several nurses were waiting for her in the emergency room. Rose stared into their eyes showing above their masks. She knew they didn't hold out much hope for the baby.

"Mrs. McCray, we're taking you up to the delivery room. Your baby is getting anxious."

Before she could ask any questions the sedative took over and she was asleep. The doctor nodded his head and they headed for the delivery room.

*****

The sun was peeping over the Blue Ridge when the ringing of the telephone broke the silence.

"Hello." Margaret's heart was beating so loudly she could barely hear Andy.

"Aunt Margaret, this is Andy. I have some news about the baby. I'm afraid it isn't good. We have a son but the doctor doesn't hold out much hope for him. His is way too early." She heard the tears in his voice.

"Andy, how is Rose?"

"She's fine, but so sad. Margaret, we named the little fellow."

"That's good. What's his name?"

"James Andrew, all three pounds of him."

There were several seconds of silence. Margaret began to cry. James took the receiver from her hand.

"Andy, repeat what you just told Margaret. She is crying."

I told her the baby's name. It is James Andrew."

"Thank you, Andy. Give Rose our love." He quietly hung up the receiver.

CHAPTER FIVE

Teresa had the plan outlined. No matter what her father wanted her to do on his list before the Will would be revealed she would do what she pleased. She had no way of knowing which man Lily would eventually marry but she would begin with Doug. Lily appeared to be comfortable with him. And why not? They were married at one time and had a child.

"I've got to find a way to get Doug's attention." Teresa had a piece of paper in her hand and she would make a list of "To Dos" to accomplish her plan. It was obvious to her that Doug had a weakness for women. She had heard rumors he had been unfaithful to Lily which had resulted in divorce. That was enough for her to come up with a plan.

Teresa dressed with meticulous care, making certain she looked her best. Wearing a new cologne, she almost felt as if she was as pretty as Lily. She had no way to know how Lily felt about herself. She had so much Teresa didn't, a profession, a child, a loving family, the list seemed endless. Accidentally finding out where Doug lived gave her one step ahead in her little game. She had eavesdropped at a gathering at Bittersweet a few weeks back. Doug's address would serve her well. She knew the area and it would be easy to hide and wait for him. Following him would be a snap; he had no idea what make of car she drove. She could hardly wait to tail him. Even as a little girl, playing detective was her favorite pretend game.

Teresa parked far enough down the street from Doug's apartment where he wouldn't notice the ugly old car. Only ten minutes had passed when he came out the front door. But something was wrong. Doug was dressed in casual clothes and was carrying something in his arms. A child? Of course, it was Anna Rose. She had probably stayed with her Dad to give Lily some rest. He seemed a kind ex-husband. Maybe she could use that to her advantage. She could deal with a baby a lot easier than her mother. But it probably wouldn't work today. He must have an important appointment and was probably taking her home, but why was he dressed so casually? Teresa's mind went into high gear. She would continue to follow him wherever he went. Maybe her time would come.

JAMES ANDREWS MCCRAY

"Such an impatient little red head!" The evening nurse had not been introduced to the newest and smallest resident of the nursery. When she saw babies that small her mind automatically saw them as hopeless.

Reading the name on the bassinet, she realized this was Rose's and Andy's baby. "Oh, little one, why were you in such a hurry? You have so much to live for."

As she checked the oxygen level in the incubator she looked up and saw the frightened young parents searching her face for just a hint of optimism. She managed a smile, then quickly turned away.

"Andy, we need to go to the chapel and pray. As a nurse, I know too much. I could see that my co-worker, Miss Reed isn't optimistic. Prayer is all we have left."

Rose and Andy turned and with arms interlocked, slowly made their way down the hall as if they were carrying the load of the world on their shoulders. And to them, they were.

*****

As she reached for the alarm, Lily instantly felt the dread depression of another day without Tom. She knew this day would be difficult, more so than the previous one. She was returning to work. There would be condolences and sad faces from fellow workers. She didn't know quite how she would react to their gestures of condolences but maybe they wouldn't expect a lot of response from her. She felt as if she had bricks attached to her feet. What happened to her energy? How could she care for all the patients on her floor? She had choices but she knew the day would be long.

Opening the door to Anna Rose's room, she remembered that Doug had agreed to keep her one more night. It really wasn't necessary but she knew he needed to feel like he was helping her. She missed the baby although she knew it was good she could spend more time with her Daddy. How Doug had changed since he came back into their lives. He was a good father.

Traffic was heavy this morning and Lily had to keep her mind on the other drivers. She wanted to think about Rose and Andy and the tiny new baby. She prayed that he would make it. Rose and Andy would be devastated if they lost their son. She didn't know how well Rose would handle that kind of grief but she prayed they would never have to know. She would have to find the time to go to Johnston City to see her dearest friends.

Pulling into the parking lot, Lily automatically looked for David's car. Secretly she hoped it wasn't there. She didn't know what to say or how to respond if he asked to see her. In her grief she knew that Tom was the one she would have married. Some of her friends would probably question that but she had no doubt in her heart. David had come to the apartment once since Tom was killed but she had been in no state to talk. He had brought food and a sympathy card.

Having no time to stop and chat, she nodded her head to the volunteer at the information desk and moved quickly to the elevator. Lily had been away only a week but it seemed strange to be back. She hoped that her duties would take her mind off her sorrow. The elevator door opened and as she stepped out into her world of the surgical ward, she knew immediately something was wrong......all doors to the patients' rooms were closed as were the double doors at the end of the hallway. The stabbing ache of sorrow returned as she suspected someone had lost a loved one. As she walked to the desk she saw his feet protruding from under the counter. Without a thought for her safely, she hurried to help in any way she could. Her shiny, white shoes made contact with the spill of dark, thick blood. She wanted to scream and look away but her eyes were drawn to the floor and the man's mutilated face. To her horror she recognized him as the husband of a young woman who had

34

terminal cancer. Why had he chosen to end his life here in this place and in such a violent way?

CHAPTER SIX

Finding the body of Clark Parish had shaken Lily so badly she had to be given a sedative and put to bed. Although she was alone with the suicide victim for only a few seconds the trauma of the past few days came rushing back as a recurring nightmare. The police came in and secured the floor and soon everyone came out of hiding to resume their duties. Lily's co-worker's talked in whispers as if they would wake a drugged Lily who lay in a bed in room 340.

Sarah and Abe tiptoed as they entered Lily's room. Their conversation had centered around how much more could sweet, shy Lily endure? It seemed unfair but that was life. Sarah's outlook was the same about Abe's Parkinson's Disease. She hadn't always felt that way until she realized he could have another disease that was uncontrollable--perhaps cancer.

They stood beside her bed, looking into her sweet face, hoping she would wake up. Lily turned her head slightly. Taking her small hand in his, it seemed to disappear beneath Abe's large fingers, stiff and swollen from medication. Gently squeezing her hand, he saw her eyes open, a faint smile began to appear slowly as she saw her loved ones.

"I'm surprised to see you two. How long have I been asleep? Is my shift over?

Sarah couldn't stifle a laugh. "Sweetie, you have been asleep for two days!!"

"Two days! Who took my shifts and where is Anna Rose?" She tried to sit up but gave in to her weakness and fell back on the pillow.

"Don't fret. Lily, everything is under control. Someone is taking your shifts until you feel stronger. Doug was more than willing to keep Anna Rose a few more days."

"But doesn't he have to work? I hope he won't lose his job." She began to wring her hands.

"He said his boss was fine with it. Everyone understands what you've been going through this past week. You're exhausted and need to rest. If you don't you won't be able to do all those things you normally do. I didn't mean to sound preachy, Lily." Sarah bent and kissed her on the forehead.

"I need to learn to say thanks and let it go at that. Don't I?"

Abe laughed. "That would be refreshing!"

*****

Rose felt the chill in the air and thought about Falls in the past. She had always loved this time of year with Thanksgiving and its wonderful foods, the trees dressed in their most brilliant colors for autumn. They had held on longer this year because of the warm weather. There had been some wonderful gatherings at the Keller Estate and later at Bittersweet. James, as the Keller's butler and right hand man, knew the proper ways to entertain and Aunt Margaret as his assistant made it a winning team.

But this morning there was a pall hanging over Rose's world. Little James Andrew was not doing well and the doctor wanted to see her this morning. It was her decision not to tell Andy about the doctors call. He had an early morning court case and his presence would not affect their son's condition. She did feel some pangs of guilt but she would tell Andy soon enough. She wished Lily were here.

It was difficult to find a parking space in the hospital lot this morning. As a nurse, Rose, felt empathy for the one she was truly concerned about. James Andrew. That tiny human being who was so anxious to come into the world came much too soon. Tears ran down her cheeks as she punched the button for the second floor.

Her heart beat faster the closer she came to the nursery. Standing over her son's bassinet was Dr. Edwards, chart in hand. Turning, he saw her standing there. He closed the chart, smiled and motioned for her to go to the nurse's station. Her knees felt rubbery and she hoped she could make it to the desk.

"Good morning, Mrs. McCray. Your husband couldn't make it, I see?" He looked puzzled.

"He had a court date and I wanted to hear what you have to say first. He might not understand." She knew he wasn't buying it.

Well, if you make a decision he will have to give his permission, too." He saw the color drain from her face.

"Mrs. McCray, I called you here today for what I hope is a positive decision. You look as if you expected bad news."

"I'm afraid I did. Do you have some good news for me?" The doctor saw just a hint of a smile on Rose's face."

"I hope it is. I have a friend who is a neonatal specialist in Nashville. He has been doing some things with preemies lately that have been saving lives."

The hint of a smile became a full-fledged one. Rose had a ray of hope for the first time since the baby was born.

*****

Teresa was an impetuous young woman. Her patience was wearing thin with her father's list of instructions. She wanted to find his Will above anything in her life. Lily didn't deserve to be a part of her father's estate and she would do her best to see that she wasn't. Just the thought of sharing with Lily made her angry.

Now that she had a plan to get Doug's attention she felt more confident in keeping Lily from getting any of her Father's estate.

Why couldn't she go through Lily and save some of the charade? But Lily was such a goody-two-shoes she wouldn't do anything to hurt someone if it could be avoided. This would take some thinking and planning on her part. Teresa thought that she was smarter than Lily . Or so she had been led to believe by observing how Lily had handled her marriage. She didn't appear to be a fighter. Teresa knew for certain that if she had been married to Doug and another woman tried to take him, she would fight with everything she had. She wondered if Lily had truly loved Doug. If she did, why didn't she fight harder?

Teresa decided that a visit to the grieving Lily was in order. After all she had kept the food delivery a secret and maybe it would help her cause if Lily knew that she could be charitable. What could her dead father do about her breaking part of the deal? Nothing.

"Hello, may I speak to a nurse on the second floor?" Teresa decided to go the direct way. Maybe she would even get Lily.

"Second floor, Mrs. Lawson speaking." She got her.

"Lily? This is Teresa. I was trying to track you down to see how you are doing after that terrible tragedy." Those kind words did not come easy for Teresa.

"This is my first day back at work after a little problem here three days ago and it feels somewhat strange but I will be fine. Where are you Teresa?" The weariness came through in her voice.

"I'm home and I have been thinking so much about you lately. Why don't I bring some supper over to your place someday this week and we can have a nice chat? I would love to see that beautiful baby of yours again." Teresa was nearly choking on her words.

She heard the hesitation but Lily was a lady.

"Of course. Give me a call the day before and we'll look forward to seeing you. I must get back to work now. Thanks for calling, Teresa."

Teresa placed the receiver gently in the holder and sat down in her father's old recliner. Lily, you're so gullible.

****

"James, does the trip to Johnston City seem longer than it used to?" Margaret and James made this trip many times to see a cousin of his who invited them on holidays and long week-ends. She had passed away about five years ago and they had stopped coming, not even to see Rose and Andy. They seemed to want to come to Bristol and be with their families.

Today would be a treat if James Andrew were healthy. Their first time seeing the little fellow was filled with fear of the unknown, the finest knit. She hoped it would fit for his trip home from the hospital. Her silent prayer was that this would happen one day soon.

"Margaret, do you remember the day you went to the bus station to pick up Rose?"

"I'll never forget that day. I think I was more nervous and scared than Rose and she was just twelve years old. She got off the bus and I wasn't there to meet her. She came into the station looking for someone she had only seen a picture of. I was looking for a girl who looked like my brother or sister-in-law. We were both surprised when we realized who each other was. I was rummaging through my purse looking for a misplaced key and she guessed that I might be her Aunt Margaret. "I saw her staring at me and those eyes! I knew she was my niece. I said, "Rose, is that you Rose?"

Then those beautiful dark eyes lit up. "I didn't recognize you. I thought you would be….." and her voice trailed off. She saw my smile and then she laughed. I said I thought you would look older and you thought I would look younger." Then we both laughed and we have been the closest of friends from that evening on. I know technically she is my niece but she is my daughter and best friend, besides you, of course.

James laughed. "I'm not jealous. I marvel at the closeness you two have enjoyed over the years."

42

She is your daughter, too. She loves you with all her heart. Giving the baby your name is proof of that."

"Yes, that is a special honor. I'm remembering another day and that is the first day you came to work for the Keller's." Margaret could feel his smile.

"Now, you are really going back. I was only a child then. Can you believe I ran away at fifteen and found a job here?

"It is hard to imagine. I couldn't see Rose doing that. Or Lily. I fell in love with you that first day."

"I had no idea. It was a shock when John let me know he had a crush on me."

"Some crush! It wasn't long after that you were married. I was deeply hurt. But look at us now. Let's not think about the past." He felt for her hand .

"You kept your feelings a deep secret. How was I to know? But maybe it wouldn't have worked out then. After all I was so young. I will admit it now that I'm an old woman but the wealth and everything that went with it was a big part of my feelings toward John Keller."

"I have always understood that and I never let it cloud my feelings for you. I'm so thankful I hung in there."

She squeezed his hand. "So am I."

*****

Rose and Andy were waiting in the lobby of the bustling hospital. They had been waiting for only a few minutes when they saw Margaret and James enter the double doors.

"Oh, Aunt Margaret, It's so good to see you." The two women held each other until Andy gently touched Margaret's arm and with his eyes asked for her embrace. She felt his body shake with the sobs that he must have been holding for weeks.

"Has something happened to the baby?" She kept her voice to a whisper.

"No, he seems to be holding his own. I've just wanted you and James here for Rose and for me, too. You're such a strong person and we'll feel stronger now that you are here."

"You're so kind, Andy. I hope James and I will help you through some of these hard times.

"You know, James is tough as nails." She laughed and reached to give James' cheek a little tweak.

Slipping between her aunt and James, Rose took their arm and marched them toward the elevators. Andy, with a quicker step than he had had in weeks, followed close behind

CHAPTER SEVEN

Lily had just walked in the door when the phone rang. Thinking it might be Aunt Margaret calling from Johnston City, she rushed to answer it. She was surprised to hear Patsy's voice on the other end. The thought had crossed her mind that she might not hear from Tom's mother again. Although Patsy's affection toward her had come as somewhat of a surprise.

"Hello, this is Lily."

"Lily, how are you, my dear?" Her voice was soft and hesitant.

"Patsy, how nice to hear your voice. How are you?" Lily really did like Tom's mother. In some ways they were so much alike, especially now that they had suffered the loss of a loved one.

"I guess I'm okay. I seem to miss Tom more every day. It's supposed to get easier. Am I right? Is that the way you feel?"

Lily wasn't sure if she really wanted to answer that question.

"I'm not certain how I feel. So many things have happened since Tom's death that I feel numb. ..not the way I want it.

"Lily, the main reason I'm calling is that Tom left a Will. They encouraged everyone in his line of work to have one. The Will is being read in the morning at 9:oo a.m. at the lawyer's office. His name is Kenneth Clark on Locust Street. I would encourage you to go because Tom told me he put you in the will."

I'm in Tom's Will?" He had never said anything to her about it.

"Of course I'll be there. I'm in shock."

"If you think about it it's not unusual. You and he would have gotten married. He wanted to be prepared for that."

"Of course you're right. I had never thought about things like that. I'll see you in the morning, Patsy." She gently replaced the receiver.

*****

They would be hard pressed to find someone at such late notice but she felt an unexplainable urge to be at the lawyer's office at 9:00. She called three co-workers before a friend on second shift agreed to trade. Lily felt guilty about missing so much work.

Quickly checking her make-up, Lily was satisfied she had not used too much blusher and mascara. As a general duty nurse she seldom wore make-up and found it daunting to apply. But today she was pleased with herself. Lily hurried to her car and the lawyer's office on Locust Street.

The traffic was heavy for a Tuesday morning. Usually by this hour she had been on duty for a couple of hours and was unaware of the traffic generated by workers who went in later. She could appreciate a little more the quietness of an earlier commute as someone cut in front of her causing her to brake suddenly.

She walked into the attorney Kenneth Clark's office at exactly 9:00 o'clock. The secretary was holding the inner office door for Patsy to enter.

46

"Good morning, Lily. Just in time." Tom's mother seemed to have aged since the funeral only a few days ago.

"Hello, Patsy. I'm not used to so much traffic. I should have left earlier." Lily prided herself on punctuality.

"You're okay. I'm nervous about this and I don't know why."

"You've been through so much lately. Everything is a different experience. I think you're holding up well." Lily didn't believe all that but Patsy needed some positive words.

Just barely seated, Lily and Patsy were surprised when Mr. Kenneth Clark entered. They had both expected a much younger man.

"Morning, ladies. I know the reading of a Will is usually not a happy occasion but I think today will be different." His presence seemed to fill the air with electricity immediately drawing the women's attention.

The distinguished, well dressed man appeared pleased with himself. Comfortable in his own skin. Both women were wondering how Tom chose him. Could they have been friends? Lily found herself strangely drawn to this man who could have been her grandfather. She didn't remember either of her grandfathers. Mr. Clark kept his eyes on Lily. If he looked toward Patsy, Lily wasn't aware of it.

Opening his shiny, leather briefcase, he placed a document on the mahogany surface of a large desk. He sat down and pulled the chair under the desk in one quick movement. He cleared his throat.

Attorney Clark began to read from the document. Lily wasn't hearing words but the soothing tone of his voice, the rhythm of a lyrical poem. Then she heard sound come from Patsy and she averted her eyes to the grieving woman. Patsy was smiling and tears were slowly making little paths down her cheeks.

"Lily, did you hear that?" She reached for Lily's hand. "Can you believe Tom was so mature for his age? To think he wanted to provide for his mother and his future wife in case of his death. I can't believe he was thinking of such serious matters."

"You had a wise and thoughtful son. You should feel proud."

"I've known that for a long time, Mr. Clark. But there is no amount of money in the world that would take his place."

Mrs. Williams and Mrs. Lawson you will each receive a check from Tom's life insurance for $50,000 in a few days. The majority of his personal items will go to Patsy, his mother. There are a few items in a special box which goes to Anna Rose Lawson, child of Mrs. Lily Lawson. Opening a desk drawer he took out a small wooden jewelry box. Lily gasped. It was the one she had chosen for her birthday gift three days before Tom was killed. Mr. Clark handed the box to Lily and she thought she saw tears in his eyes. Lily gently touched it's smooth finish and cried.

"Mrs. Lawson, you'll be interested in it's contents." He wanted to take her into his arms.

"Would you open it, please I'm shaking too much?"

Taking the beautifully crafted wooden box from Lily, he slowly opened it. A shiver ran through her whole body. In a flash she saw Tom's face. Why had Tom had her birthday gift ready to be given to her the day the Will was read? And why did he put Anna Rose's name on the jewelry box?

Then she realized that Patsy was trying to tell her something. It all seemed like a dream.

"Lily, I haven't told you this before because I didn't think you would believe me. The night before Tom died he brought this box into my bedroom and asked if I would do him a favor. Of course I said yes. He said if anything happened to him before Lily's birthday, please give this to her.

I laughed and said that you know I will but why are you thinking that way?

An expression of sadness spread slowly over his kind face. His eyes were filled with tears and I began to cry. He took me in his arms and told me not to worry, he was just being cautious. He loved you, Lily, and Anna Rose so much. Knowing that you were alone he wanted to provide what he could if something happened to him. I don't know what is in the box but I would guess it is worth quite a lot of money.

"Mrs. Lawson, Why don't you open the box?" Lily thought she saw tears in his dark eyes but she wasn't absolutely certain.

Without a word she clicked the bronze lock to open the lid. Inside the box was a small black velvet ring box. Lily's hand trembled as she lifted it and held it a second. It was as if everyone took in a breath at the same time. The hinges on the small box were taut and it took some effort to bring it back far enough to see the contents. Just at that moment the sun broke through the clouds and sent a ray through the window of Attorney Clark's office. The three persons staring at the little ring box gasped at the same moment. The large diamond ring sent rays of light from every facet giving it a star-like quality. No one spoke for several minutes.

"He must have saved for many years to buy that." Lily found her voice.

Patsy's sobs were uncontrollable. She knew Tom was a special person but she had no idea how much he loved Lily and Anna Rose.

CHAPTER EIGHT

She stopped again to look at the map. The town of Masonberg should be here where the two roads crossed. There was nothing but trees and grass, not one building. Teresa must have looked at the numbers wrong. Masonberg could not hide behind a tree. From the data in her father's dog-eared atlas there were about one thousand people who called Masonberg home. Where had she gone wrong?

Teresa drove on several miles until she saw a service station in the distance. She knew someone was there who could clear up this whole matter. As she pulled up close to the front door of the tiny gas station she noticed an old man sitting on a bench just outside the door. At first he didn't look up. Probably taking a nap, she guessed. Stopping the car, turned off the engine. Still no response. She could stand it no longer. Slowly opening the car door she stepped out onto the graveled lot. He did not make a move nor look up.

"Mister, I need to ask you a question. You see, I'm lost. I need to find Masonberg, Virginia". Still no response.

"Mister, maybe you didn't hear me but I need to know where I missed the turn to Masonberg." There was impatience in her voice.

Slowly he raised his head and looked her straight in the eye. "I heered ye the first time. Masonburg is no more. It's not there." Teresa thought she saw tears in his faded blue eyes.

"How could that be? Was there a fire, an explosion? What made it disappear? How long ago was that?" She began to wonder if she were dreaming. She stared at the old man, who had turned to walk away.

"Mister, please don't go. It's really important I know what happened to the town of Masonburg. I really have to know." She hated to beg.

He turned and raised his head and looked at Teresa with such fright in his eyes that she knew something had gone terribly wrong.

"Lady, I don't know who you are but I wish you would leave me be. Go ask somebody else about what happened to Masonberg. I ain't gonna tell ye." And with that he walked back into his greasy little gas station.

Teresa, realizing he was a lost cause, got in her car and started the engine. Just before she turned to enter the road she saw a head covered in white hair peek around the corner of the tiny building. At first she thought it was a girl but when the little person came into full view, she saw that it was a boy with long hair.

"Lady, what are you doin here? I heerd you say something about Masonberg. My grandpa is a little off his rocker. Happened about the time a gas tank exploded just a few feet away. He can't hear too good neither." He turned his head and spat a stream of dark brown liquid. Teresa's eyes were drawn to the circle of tobacco juice being slowly absorbed into the red soil.

"Can you hear me, girl. I said what are you doing here?" His voice had more authority than most other boys his age.

"I asked you where Masonberg is and that's all you need to know. Teresa was tired and wanted to finish this project and go home.

"You act like the town is lost. It's right over them hills there. People get the road numbers mixed up. This here one is called number 31 and you want 32." He may as well have added, 'stupid girl' for that's the tone which came through.

"Thank you and now can you tell me the shortest way to get to that road?"

"I knowed it. I might as well ride along with you so you won't get lost." He headed for her car.

Teresa knew she had met her match. Oh, well, what could it hurt. The boy was no more than ten years old although he had the presence of someone much older.

"Okay. You win. Get in the car." She hoped she wouldn't live to regret this decision.

*****

The beautiful diamond ring was securely placed in a safety deposit box until Lily was certain her home had a secure place for Tom's extravagant gift to her and Anna Rose. She could not guess its worth and the attorney, Mr. Clark, suggested that he and Lily go to the jeweler's place and find out. Her feelings were ambivalent about this excursion with almost a total stranger. One part of her was drawn to this man she had never seen before.

She told herself she must not let these thoughts enter her mind. She hoped she could keep that promise but she had never felt about anyone in this way, not even Tom.

She would put it out of her mind. She had too many things to deal with now. Anna Rose was becoming a person in her own right. She was so much like her father that it was scary.

"I know she needs to spend more time with children her own age." Lily remarked to Rose just recently. Rose had brought baby James to spend the day with her and Anna Rose. He was growing so fast the two friends joked that he would soon be Anna Rose's size if not her age. The two childhood friends, now mothers, felt closer than they had in many years.

Lily's thoughts always went back to Rose whenever she had a problem. There was no way she would confess her thoughts about lawyer Clark to her closest friend. She couldn't imagine what Rose would think of her illicit thoughts.

She must decide what to do about the ring. Would Tom want her to sell it and open a savings account? Should she keep it in a safe place unitl Anna Rose was older? Or maybe when she was ready for college? She needed to talk to someone. Abe! Why hadn't she thought of him before. Dear, calm, practical Abe. He would give her the good advice she needed and she would listen.

He answered on the second ring.

"Hello." His voice was very soft. Lily knew this as a Parkinson symptom.

"Hello, Abe. How is my favorite dad?" She heard his laugh

"Lily, it's been too long since I've heard that sweet voice. I'm doing as well as an old man with Parkinson's can do."

"This is my day off and I wonder If I can come over and talk awhile?"

"I can't wait. I'll make us a sandwich for lunch. Is peanut butter and banana still a favorite?" She heard the excitement in his voice. She knew he had good days and bad…this must be a good one.

CHAPTER NINE

"This is it? This is Masonberg? Nothing more than a wide spot in the road."

"You got it. Never did mount to much. Who you wanna see in this place? Must be somebody important but I cain't think of anyone like that here." He had the mannerisms of an old man and spoke with unusual authority for one so young.

"I don't really want to go into the whole story why I need to find a Mr. John Mason."

The corners of his mouth turned up in an expression between a slight smile and a smirk.

"How about somebody else, maybe a Sam Jones?"

"Sam Jones won't do. It has to be John Mason." She was afraid she was on a wild goose chase. Teresa looked down the empty street running through the middle of town, searching for some place to find an answer to her question. In the distance she thought she saw an American flag....maybe a post office. The disheveled young boy was off like a shot, not waiting for Teresa to open the car door. She started to call to him and realized she hadn't asked his name.

The boy disappeared into a small white building. Child-like printing in black paint over the door spelled out Post Office, Masonberg, Va. So there really is a Masonberg, Virginia. The old screen door was riddled with holes reminding Teresa of the one at her grandmother's house she had visited only once. Every time she asked her mother when were they going back for a visit, the answer was always, "soon," but they never did.

The tiny building was dark and smelled of dampness. The boy was at the counter talking to a matronly woman who seemed distracted by a stack of mail resting on the counter.

As Teresa walked up behind the boy she heard him say, "I don't think she really knows who it is she wants but do you have any Masons around here?" Something about the question caused her to look at the dirty little boy and smile.

"Masons in Masonberg! Well wouldn't that be a coincidence? And the funny thing is that the last Mason died just about three months ago. His name was John.

Teresa's heart almost stopped. Now, what will I do?

"Miss, I couldn't help but overhear what you said about the last Mason dying. Did he by any chance have any family, children maybe?"

"I can't think of any right off hand but maybe old Miss Crawford down the road apiece could tell you. Some people round here say she is near a hundred years old but I don't think she has been seen since her ninety year birthday. She just looks old. If anyone would know about the Masons she would. Heard she was about to marry one of them when she was young. Seems he went off to the war and never returned. Sad!" She began to sort the mail on the counter.

"Thank you." There was just a slight nod of the head from the post- mistress.

Teresa headed for the door and the boy asked if he could come along. She nodded her head and he smiled as he hurried to catch up.

"Which way is this woman's house?" She looked at the boy walking beside her. She couldn't quite say why they seemed to be a team.

"It's not fer around the curve down there. I hear she is a nice lady but I never seen her before."

"Well I guess we'll find out soon enough."

They walked along for a few minutes in silence. She coughed and cleared her throat.

"What would you be doing if you weren't walking along with me?" She knew he must have a reason for choosing to stick to her like glue.

"I don't really know. Seems we both needed a friend and you were there."

Just then a little mountain cabin came into view. Smoke was coming from the stone chimney, curling its way into the blue mountain sky, The house was very small with a front porch just big enough for two rocking chairs. A single pot of red geraniums was the only other item.

"Should we go and knock on the door?" This coming from the little boy.

"I don't know any other way to get her attention. Don't think throwing rocks would do any good."

"Let's try….. Miss Crawford. You have company."

Not a sound came from the house.

The boy made a dash for the door. Just as he raised his hand to knock, it flew open.

"Who is out here making so much noise?" Her voice was strong for a ninety something old woman.

"Just me, Jimbo and this young lady. She's lookin' fer a man by the name of Mason, John Mason."

Her expression changed from one of questioning to one of shock. "If you know what's good for you young woman, you'll just turn around and go back where you come from." With that she stepped across the threshold and slammed the door.

"Teresa stood there with her mouth open. "I didn't even get to say a word to her. That John Mason must not be one of her favorite people."

"Guess not. Whatcha gonna do now?"

"I wish I knew---go home, I guess--but I really do need to find this John Mason." Teresa looked at the boy as if to say, come on and get in the car.

*****

"That was the best peanut butter and banana sandwich I ever ate." Lily blotted her mouth with Sarah's snow white linen napkin.

"You're just saying that to make an old man feel good. It wasn't even a good banana." He laughed that spontaneous, wake you up laugh that only Abe could do.

"You make me feel good when I hear you laugh. It truly was good. Now I need to talk to you about something." She saw the mirth leave Abe's eyes. He expected her to say something very serious. He would be pleasantly surprised at her question.

"Lily, I'll listen to anything you have to tell me.' He reached over and patted her hand.

60

"It's really not bad, just something I need some advice about." She reached into her purse and took out the ring box.

"Abe, Tom's Will was read yesterday and a puzzling thing happened, The lawyer handed me this pretty wooden jewelry box Tom had planned to give me for my birthday. I nearly passed out and then he said to open it. Oh, I forgot the box had Anna Rose's name on it. My hands were shaking as I took it from Mr. Clark. I opened the box and inside was a velvet ring box. In that was the most beautiful diamond ring you can imagine. When I came to my senses I asked him if there was a letter with the box. He shook his head, no." Lily looked into Abe's soft eyes and waited for his reaction. The Parkinson's had taken its toll on his response. Before he became ill he was quick with an answer.

"Lily, what is the problem? You have lost a loving and caring man who made plans for you and Anna Rose if something should happen to him. I'm going to ask you a question but you don't have to answer if you think it is too personal.

"I would never think that of you. We're family. Go ahead."

"Had you told Tom you would marry him?" He took her small hand stroking it with his puffy one. She smiled ever so faintly.

"No, but I think if he had asked me again, I would have said, yes. I realize now, too late, that I loved him very much." Her tears began to fall gently on his hand. He took her into his tremoring arms, resting her head on his shoulder, They both wept.

"Sweetheart, keep the ring at the bank in a safe deposit box until you need the money and hopefully that will be a long time. Maybe when Anna Rose starts to college. That brought a smile from Lily.

"Now that we have that settled, I have something to talk to you about. I'm afraid it is a little more serious than a diamond ring. Have you been around Margaret lately?'

"I'm sorry to say I haven't. I saw her for just a minute at Tom's services. With all I had on my mind I did think she was a little distant to me." She saw the worried look in his eyes.

"That's just one symptom. She is so forgetful and you know that is not like Margaret. And James is worried sick. Rose won't listen to anything he says. She wants to believe her Aunt needs a change of scenery and she will be good as new."

"You want me to talk to Rose?"

"Please, James is almost sick with worry. We just can't get through to her".

"I'll see what I can do."

"Thanks, that's all we can expect."

CHAPTER TEN

Teresa rolled down her window, wondering if the smell of Jimbo's unwashed body would ever leave. Jimbo, what a name! Who would call a child that? She kind of felt sorry for him, as much as she would allow herself. Teresa was never known for trying to walk in someone else's shoes. Her own daddy had called her selfish many times. She thought this was probably the reason for this wild goose chase. That's just what it was. She would never find this John Mason and, therefore, she would never find her father's Will. But she must and she believed her father wanted her to find it after she did a few things to prove that she was worthy.

"Miss Upity, you're awfully quiet. Are you mad at me?"

She didn't dare look into those big blue eyes of his. She had always had a weakness for eyes the color of the sky on a clear spring day. She thought it could have been because she had always been kidded about her black eyes.

"Mad? What did you do that made me mad? It takes a lot to get me upset." She knew that wasn't true. Why did she tell lies at the drop of a hat?

I thought you might blame me for the lady turning you away. She might have talked to you if it weren't for me." He took a deep breath and looked down at his bare feet.

"No, there's something about John Mason that is dark and she doesn't want to be reminded of it.

"We gotta find out what that is about her. I bet someone knows. Come on I got an idee."

"Tell me where we're going. I don't know this part of Virginia. I wish I did."

"Just keep on going until I say turn. You got a ways yet." His countenance changed and he looked thrilled to be showing her the way to somewhere she needed to go.

They rode on a few minutes in silence. Teresa could stand it no longer.

"Do you really know where we're going or is this just a wild goose chase?"

"I know, alright. I don't know why I didn't think of this before. Mr. Mason had a daughter who lives just a little ways down this here road. She is kind of different but who ain't? She never married and you can guess what people have said over the years. I don't know anything about her but that sometimes she doesn't act like normal folks. I heerd that Mr. Mason, her old man, was very disappointed about her. Never could seem to make a lady out of her. I don't know what her mother thought. It 's really not too swift to go against your parents."

"Slow down, Miss. The road is comin' up fast on your right.

Teresa braked quickly, dust left a trail behind her car.

It's a little house, no, it's just a shack. Some old man, farmhand, had lived there until he died. Mr. Mason's daughter moved right in. It sure beat living on the street. When her daddy found out she was living in the cabin, he swallowed his pride and went to see her. He found it hard to believe she was living in a shack that barely gave her shelter from the rain. The story goes that he begged and pleaded with her , crying all the time. That was not like him. All his words could not break through her

64

stubbornness and she refused to go with him. He left with a broken heart."

"A Sad Story"

The two traveling companions rode along in silence for several miles. Then with a very quiet voice, Jimbo asked Teresa a question. "Do you really like me?"

The seemingly tough, street smart girl was at a loss for words. She hesitated too long before she answered.

"Well, I got my answer. You think I'm just a smelly kid and you put up with me because you want me to help you find John Mason, right?"

"Wrong. I do like you but you took me off guard. You would be easier on the nose if you had a good bath but I've had times like that. I haven't said anything because I'm sure you would do better if you could."

"Thank you, I guess. You're right, I'll take a bath as soon as I can. Slow down I believe it's the next turn."

Teresa barely made the turn onto a narrow dirt road not much wider than a path. Jimbo had fallen against the door.

"Ouch! That door handle is sharp!"

"Sorry."

"I think her place should come up in just a minute.

Before the sound could leave the car, there it was . Not much to look at, the crumbling shack had probably never seen a coat of paint. There was a front stoop with room for an old caned bottom chair. A shiver went through Teresa as she thought of living in such a hut.

"Pull up there to the porch and I'll see if somebody's home." Teresa hesitated as if she feared getting too close to the dreary little shack. As she inched closer she watched for signs of life.

Opening his door, Jimbo was out in a flash and on the little porch. He knocked on the side of the rusty screen door. Not a sound from within. He knocked again, much louder.

Teresa spied the end of the gun poking through a hole in the screen.

"Jimbo watch out. There's a gun."

He hit the floor as fast as a well trained trooper. Looking up he saw the outline of an old woman, her hair in a knot atop her head.

"Don't shoot lady, alls we wanted to do was to ask you a question".

Lowering the gun just a few inches, she looked at him as if he were no more important than a house fly. The scars covering her face were frozen in place. Jimbo could not read her expression. He turned and leapt from the tiny stoop.

Come back here, boy. What do you want to know?" She lowered the gun and sat in the only chair in sight.

"Yes, ma'am. Promise not to point that gun at me again?"

"Sorry, I would never make such a promise, especially to a stranger like you."

"Okay." Inching just a little closer, he stood there ready to ask her the question"

"What about your girlfriend in the car?

"My girlfriend! She ain't my girl friend. I'm just helping' her find somebody."

"And you think I might know where this someone might be?"

"Well, here goes--she wants to know if you know a man by the name of John Mason." Even through the scars he could see the color fade from her grotesque face.

Tightening the grip on her gun, she stood up and pointed the muzzle at his head.

"Get off my property and take that nosey girl with you. I'll have no doings with such as her."

Jimbo scrambled to his feet and headed for the car.

"Get out of here as fast as you can. That's a mean white woman. She knowed old John, okay. She almost passed out when I asked her the question."

"I'm sorry she scared you. How are we going to find this man? I need to start for home but I need to talk to him. Where to now, my friend?"

"Well, I don't know girls very well but I'm hungry as a bear. Maybe we could go back to that little store and get something to eat. Do you have any money? I have a little change I can offer."

"I think we can scrape up enough to buy something," She gave the old car more gas as they entered the main road. She hoped she could start back to Bristol soon.

They made a strange pair.....this young woman who carried herself with an air of importance and this unkempt, barefoot, stinky boy. They looked over the shelves filled with snacks, finally settling on two packs of crackers and a large bottle of soda pop. The middle aged woman at the counter wondered if they planned to drink from the same bottle. The young lady didn't appear to be that type.

"Ma'am, would you happen to have a paper cup we could buy for a penny or two?" Teresa gave her a smile which came rarely from her.

"I just happen to have one I'll give you. Where are you two headed? Don't believe I've seen you around these parts before." She brushed her graying hair from her forehead, revealing beads of perspiration.

"Jimbo, here lives a few miles down the road and I'm from the Bristol area. I'm here to try to find a person or something about him. So far I haven't had any luck. I'll take that back,....I did find out he was dead. I guess I won't find out any information and just go on home."

"Who might you be looking for? I was born and raised here and I know just about everybody."

"His name is John Mason. I need to ask him how he knew my Dad."

"John Mason! I went to school with him. Didn't spend much time with him after we finished school but I kept up with everyone in my class. I never heared any thing bad about him. Let me see who might know him. Yes, he was good friends with Bill Link. He lives not far from here. Do you want me to call him and see if you could come over?"

"Would you do that? Sure would appreciate it." She was beginning to feel better about her search.

While the lady at the counter made the call the two hungry travelers ate their meager snacks.

The lady returned the receiver to the cradle and turned with a beaming face.

"Bingo! He said to come on over. What happened to your snacks? My, you must have been hungry."

*****

The little yellow house was a breath of fresh air after seeing all the crumbling shacks dotting the countryside. This time they both went to the door. A black and white dog was asleep on the porch. Slowly he opened one eye and observed the intruders. He must have figured they were not worth a bark and closed his eye to resume his nap.

Before they could knock, the door opened to reveal an elderly man with snow white hair. His clothes were clean and there was even a crease down the middle of his jean pants.

Lowering his glasses he peered at the odd couple.

"Could I help you ?" Such a soft voice for a man his size. Teresa knew right away she liked him.

"Yes sir. I hope so. I need to find out some information about John Mason. We were told you were a friend." She saw the sadness cloud his blue eyes.

"Yes, John was my best friend. You do know he has passed away?"

"Yes, I was sorry to hear that but maybe you can tell me what I need to know."

"Come in the house." Holding the door he motioned to a room on the right of the dark hallway. Teresa was surprised to see a cozy little room with a couch and two chairs with cheery flowered upholstery. It looked like a room a woman would have furnished.

"Do you live here alone?" She had to ask.

"I do now. My wife passed away about six months ago. I certainly do miss her. Please have a seat. May I get you a cold drink or a glass of water?"

Jimbo, who had been quiet up until now spoke.

"Some cold water would be good. It sure has been hot today." He hoped that would explain his not so pleasant odor.

"I'll be right back."

"I wish he had offered us something to eat. The crackers are long gone." Teresa shook her head in agreement.

It was just a few minutes until the host returned. He was carrying a tray filled with glasses of water and bread with a jar of jam.

"I thought maybe you two would like a little something to eat." He did not miss the smiles on the faces of the two young guests.

After they were settled with a chunk of homemade bread slathered in strawberry jam he asked Teresa what was the big question she had for him.

Teresa had not told Jimbo everything about the question she wanted to ask the elderly man. His eyes were frozen on her. He had given this much thought but still could not imagine what could be so important.

Clearing her throat, changing her position to get a better view of the old man's face, she opened her mouth to speak. Suddenly an earth shaking scream came from somewhere in the little house. Jimbo fell to the floor and covered his head with his hands. Teresa sat frozen, unable to move. The man jumped up and ran into the adjoining room. It seemed longer but in a few seconds Jimbo unclasped his hands and looked searchingly at Teresa. Shaking her head was all she could do. Her mouth was too dry to speak. Just then the man came back into the room looking as if he had seen a ghost.

I think I'm going to have to ask you to leave now. Maybe we can meet somewhere away from here. How about the store just down the road?

"When could you do that? I really need to head home to Bristol." She had suddenly found her voice.

The old man looked puzzled but finally found his voice. "I'll be there in about thirty minutes."

"If it's longer than that I'll be gone. I don't like to drive at night alone."

"I understand that. If I cannot show up, you know that I couldn't leave here. I will do my best." With that he turned and walked with stooped shoulders into the house.

*****

Teresa and the boy waited two hours for the old man. The store closed, the lights went out. Tt was so dark they could not see their hands in front of their faces.

"I guess we'll stay here and sleep in the car. I don't know anything else to do." Teresa had always been able to come up with a workable solution. She could have gone back to Bristol but she would have been defeated in her purpose for coming here.

"I'm so hungry I could eat a cow!"

"I don't have a cow but I'll divide this honey bun with you."

"Where did you get that?" She knew he didn't have any money.

I sort of borrowed it." He laughed.

"You stole from that nice lady?"

"Nice lady! She knew we didn't have any money and she didn't offer to give us a thing to eat. I don't feel bad about taking the honey bun," He proceeded to peel the crinkly wrapper from the sticky, sugary treat. Breaking it in half, he offered a piece to Teresa. Her first thought was I can't take that from his dirty hand but her hunger won out.

"Thank you, Jimbo." She ate it, relishing every crumb of sweetness.

"I guess we should try to get some sleep. I'm going out here behind these bushes before I turn in. She knew what he meant. She had learned to hold her bathroom urges. It was simply mind over matter.

By the time Jimbo returned she had settled down in the back seat. She knew this would be a long night but it was too late to return home.

"Ain't you goin? He crawled into the front wondering what position would be most comfortable for sleep.

"I don't need to. We might as well try to get some sleep. I'm guessing the store opens early."

"For all the good it will do us. The stingy, old woman won't offer us a crumb."

"Maybe she will think about that tonight and have a change of heart." She didn't really believe that but hoped it would help the dirty young boy occupying her front seat.

As Teresa was thinking about the events of the day she heard soft snoring coming from the front seat. She couldn't help but wonder what this young boy wanted from her. He seemed straightforward enough except for stealing the honey bun but she would chalk that up to hunger. Slowly she began to feel sleep taking over her thoughts. She let herself go and soon she was out.

Teresa began to feel she was floating. Looking down she saw the tops of houses and trees…there was a lake and what looked like a ribbon of a river. Picking up speed she closed her eyes. Just as she thought she would hit the water, she came to a stop and hovered as she had seen seagulls do when they were searching for their next meal. Opening her eyes she could see the outline of a small boat, maybe a canoe. She squinted and the image became clearer. She could see that the boat contained two people… one smaller than the other. Then a strange thing happened. It was if she was seeing through binoculars and she perceived the face of the two persons. One was an older man and the other a young boy, maybe ten or twelve. She did not recognize the man but the boy looked familiar. She tried to place him but she could not. Then she heard him asking the man about what to do if he caught a fish. The voice! She knew it. IT was her father! Her father as a young boy. But who was the older man?

Teresa felt her body ascending and she knew the dream would end. But wait…off in a distance was a speed boat headed at a high rate of speed directly at the little boat and the man and boy. She tried to call out to them but no sound came from her mouth. She closed her eyes to keep from witnessing the horrible crash. Suddenly she was awake and opening the car door. The tapping had stopped. It must have been the wind. Jimbo was still asleep in the front seat. She tried to sit up and realized how stiff she had become sleeping in the cramped quarters. Deciding to wake up the dirty smelly boy, she shook his shoulder.

CHAPTER ELEVEN

The nights seemed to get longer for Lily. As a nurse she knew the danger of sleeping pills. She tried warm baths and reading but the light sleep she managed was filled with disturbing nightmares. They never changed except for the main character. She was always trying to catch up with Tom or Doug but not David. She wondered why she did not dream of the doctor.

She heard the ringing of a bell...was she still dreaming? Then came a very persistent knock. She suddenly realized this was for real. This was the morning Doug was picking up Anna Rose. How could she have slept through the alarm? Grabbing her robe from the foot of the bed she hurried down the hall.

"Coming! Her voice was raspy and she felt a slight soreness in her throat.

"How could I have overslept? Her words filtered into the hallway as she opened the door. She was surprised to see Doug dressed in his Sunday best.

"Did I forget something? Where are you and Anna Rose going today that is so special?"

Instead of answering his daughter's distraught mother, he took her in his arms and kissed her gently on the lips. Her brain was saying, "don't do this," but her body was responding to his gentle caresses. She put her arms around his chest, drawing him closer. Lily had forgotten how good he smelled. Taking her face into his strong hands he looked into her beautiful eyes and kissed here again, He saw her just the moment she began to cry.....Anna Rose was standing in the doorway, her beautiful dark eyes filled with tears.

"It's okay, sweetie." Lily started toward her daughter but Anna Rose was there in a split second, her arms wrapped tightly around her Mother's legs.

"Anna Rose, look at your Daddy. I would never hurt your Mother. I was giving her a kiss to let her know how much I love her." Just a hint of a smile appeared on the frightened little girl's face.

"Like you give me, Daddy?"

"Yes, sweetheart."

Lily tried to hold it back but the joyous laughter started deep down, filling her whole being until it burst forth releasing the sorrow, the stress, the fear and most of all the sudden renewal of her love for Doug. She laughed until the tears began and then she laughed so hard her stomach hurt. It was infectious...Doug started to laugh, and then Anna Rose joined in. Lily managed to stop for a few minutes and then it came of it's own volition. Soon all three were on the floor rolling and laughing.

When there was no more laughter in her to come out, Lily knew the answer to the question that had plagued her for over two years. The answer seemed so very plain to her now. She felt as if the laughter had been the cathartic she had needed all along. Doug was the one. Anna Rose's father. The man who loved her when she had been unlovable. Doug , the patient one. Doug, the loving father. Doug, the persistent one.

Putting her head in her hand, she looked at Doug, and said, "yes."

"I don't remember what I asked."

"Well, you haven't asked today. If the offer still stands, I'm saying, "Yes," to your question if I will marry you."

Is the question still valid?" It will remain valid for the rest of my life."

"Then, yes, I will marry you."

"Am I hearing things? Repeat that, please."

"I said if the offer is still good, I will marry you!"

He didn't answer Lily but he took her in his arms and turned her face so that he could look into her beautiful eyes.

"Don't you know that I love you more than I could ever tell you? I want to show you that I have grown up and I can be a good husband and father. You asked why I was wearing dress clothes today. I have an appointment with a banker to ask for a loan for this little cottage over on Baker Street. I want a place for Anna Rose to have plenty of room and a yard to play in. It is plenty big enough for a family of three and maybe four." Lily was smiling although her face was wet with tears. He kissed her gently. Anna Rose rushed over and tried to put her tiny arms around both her parents.

*****

"Do you think we'll get the loan?" Lily had never gone to a bank to ask for money. She felt embarrassed and uneasy.

"Yes, I believe so. You surprised him by showing up. He was only expecting me." He gave her a bear hug.

"It would be good if he would take my salary into consideration but he talked as if he wouldn't."

"That problem will be changed some day I would hope.

Since neither of us has to go to work we have time to go see this little house we're trying to buy."

"I can't wait" She took his hand and led him toward the car and the little cottage on Baker Street.

They turned down the tree lined street into a neighborhood where time seemed to have stopped in the late 40s and 50s. The homes were small but all a little different. The trees were tall and full. Lily could almost hear the voices of children as they played in the shade on a lazy summer day. One small white house with a picket fence stood out and she whispered, what number are we looking for?"

"Number 132." Her eyes quickly searched for a number. There it was, just above the blue door. 132! She couldn't believe her eyes. How perfect. More like a dream.

Doug parked directly in front of the gate. Lily was out of the car and through the gate before Doug could walk around the car. He laughed at her excitement.

"Wait on me, Mrs. Lawson. She stopped suddenly. Slowly turning to face him. Her smile radiated her excitement.

Arm and arm they walked the few steps to the little white house they both knew would be their future home.

Their thoughts were running in tandem; they couldn't wait to show the house to Anna Rose. How could life be any better?

CHAPTER TWELVE

Opening his eyes, he looked into Teresa's face and his memory was too slow to remember where he was until her voice reminded him.

She caught this body odor as he began to move. Gee, he's a dirty boy! If he is going to stay around me, it's a bath today.

"Jimbo, get up. It's late and I need to leave for home. And besides we need to find a way to mooch some breakfast."

"What? What did you say? Oh, my neck. I don't think I moved all night." He groaned and made a motion to get up,

"Maybe the store is open and you can go in and wash yourself a little or a lot. You are rank. Do that before we try to find some food."

"Yes, ma'am. You don't look so good yourself."

"Well at least I don't smell to high heaven." She scooted out of the back seat and stood up. She felt like moaning but wouldn't give Jimbo the satisfaction

"Where do you think we might find some breakfast? I don't think the woman in the store will give it to us. Do you?"

"I don't know. Maybe she softened up last night. I'll go see."

Teresa combed through her hair with her fingers before entering the store. The lighting was very dim and at first she didn't see the man behind the counter.

"Where's the lady who was here yesterday?" She asked with her sunniest smile.

"This is Mary's day off. I'm Mr. Davis, her husband. Could I help you with something?" He smiled and she noticed his yellow teeth. She thought of her Uncle Walt who had been a lover of chewing tobacco and had died of throat cancer.

Moving closer to him, she looked him in the eye. "You see, Mr. Davis, my friend Jimbo and I have this little problem. I was supposed to return to Bristol yesterday and I couldn't because I have to wait and see a man about something and I ran out of money. We certainly could use a little breakfast. Could I do some chores around here for some food? I noticed the front needs sweeping up and do you have any dishes or anything I could wash? I'm a good dishwasher." She could almost see the tears in his eyes.

"Well. Maybe we can work out something for you to do. You're right. The front needs a good sweeping How about you start with that." He was thinking that his wife would not like this but she wasn't working today. He realized someone in the family had to clean up…he certainly was not up to it.

"Thank you, Mister. I'll get that done very quickly."

He handed her a broom which had seen better days.

She went to work with vigor and soon the front entrance was clean. Motioning to Jimbo, he came running, hoping that was the signal for breakfast.

"Are we on for something to eat?"

"I hope you're included. Seeing his countenance fall, she told him not to worry, he would get some breakfast.

Just about that time the owner came out of the door.

"Looks like you did a good enough job. Come on in and I have some breakfast for you.

Teresa hesitated. "What about Jimbo, here?

"Did he help you rake leaves? If he did then he can come in, too." He knew Jimbo didn't rake a single leaf.

"He's my friend and I'll share with him."

She motioned for him to follow her into the back room.

As her eyes adjusted to the dark she was shocked to see how it had been set up like a living room with a long table at one end. On the crisp white cloth was a small feast of cereal, fruit, sweet rolls of several kinds and a pitcher of orange juice. As Teresa took this all in she began to think she was dreaming. It had been so long since she had eaten a real meal. She couldn't help salivating as her eyes went from one food to another. Jimbo, walking behind Teresa, had not seen the table. When he saw all the food he exclaimed, "Jesus, you must be getting ready for the queen!"

"Little Lady, this is for you. And your hungry guest. Enjoy!" He turned and headed back into the store.

"What did you do for him? I thought you only raked the leaves!"

"You know that is all I did, Mr. Dirty Mouth."

"Whatever. Let's eat. I'm so hungry. I could eat a horse!"

"Sorry, I don't see any horse on the table. How about some cereal and fruit instead?"

The two disheveled, smelly, young people forgot any manners they may have possessed up until that time. When the man returned an hour later, everything had been consumed. and the two diners were sound asleep. The man couldn't help but smile. Studying them a few seconds his countenance changed and in a gruff voice said, "Okay, you two gluttons, time to clear up this mess. They were up and in action in seconds. After having such a feast, the least they could do was clean up.

As they started out the door, the man called to them. "Young lady, there's someone here to see you."

Just at that moment the old man from Masonberg stepped into the room. Before Teresa could say a word, he walked toward her extending his hand mumbling something about an apology.

"Miss, I'm sorry I didn't keep our date last night. But I had mixed feelings about telling you what I know about John Mason. I spent a sleepless night and I've decided that its time to bring the secret into the light. Maybe then it can be looked at as a mistake of the heart and He forgives . I'm ready to talk.

The store owner remaining in the doorway, sighed and told Teresa and the old man to stay in the special room as long as they needed to talk.

"Come on, Jim Bob, or Bo Bo , or whatever your name might be. You can work for all that breakfast you just ate."

Jimbo made a face but followed the man to the front of the store.

The room was suddenly quiet. Teresa waited for the man to speak. After several minutes he cleared his throat and began. What a strange story he had to tell.

"Your Mother and the man you called Daddy were brother and sister…. twins actually. Have you ever known a set of twins?"

"I have not been that close to a set of twins. I can't believe what you are telling me."

"I would swear on a bible that every word is true. Now back to the story." Clearing his throat and smoothing the little bit of hair he had, he continued.

"Your Mother met a man who took advantage of young women who had money and he did the same thing to your mother. She became pregnant. In those days that was almost as bad as a death sentence. She couldn't bring herself to tell anyone, not even her twin brother.

Her twin, your father, had married Anna, and soon she was pregnant, too. Finally after your Mother thought she could hide her condition no longer she came to her brother to ask for his help. A special plan had to be worked out. Your Dad could see no other way but to leave Anna and pretend to marry his sister. Of course they had to move away where no one knew them. They moved into a mountain cabin over the mountains in Virginia. They had every intention of leaving their hide-away after you were born and given up for adoption. But plans don't always work out just like you plan. Your young Mother died in childbirth. You can imagine how distraught your father was. He went into a deep depression and was unable to care for you. A young woman, daughter of John Mason began to care for you and your father. Soon her kindness overshadowed his grief and they were married. She is the woman you have called Mother all these years. Of course to keep the secret they had to move again...this time to the Bristol area. I suspect that was to be closer to Lily and her Mother. Your natural father was killed in a car accident just before you were born. There is so much sadness in this secret story.

The woman with the scarred face, who accosted you yesterday, is your half sister. She discovered some details of the secret and made up the remainder. She is a danger to you, so stay away. John Mason, the grandfather, thought he had buried the dark secret but he was mistaken. Now you know the truth. I pray you will not let it ruin your life like it's done to others. You had a special Mother and an uncle who would have given his life for you.

CHAPTER THIRTEEN

The sun burst through the windows as if sounding an alarm. Lily opened her eyes just enough to see the face of the clock. Then she remembered the evening before. Or was it a dream? No, how could it be a dream. She had accepted Doug's proposal of marriage. Then she heard his last words as he left at almost midnight, "I'll be over early and cook breakfast for you and our daughter."

A knock on the door.

"Who is it?"

"It's your future husband, Doug."

"Oh, that one! Come in."

"Good morning, Love. Could there be another?"

"No, sweetheart. Only you."

Taking her into his arms he kissed her tenderly. What a wonderful life we're going to have."

"Having," Lily corrected "Let's get some breakfast so you can go to work."

"I know I have to keep my mind on my work but today it will be impossible. So many things have happened in the past few hours."

"Yes, and do you know what I think the first thing we have to decide?

"No, what? I know, our wedding."

"Yes, and do you know the first things we have to decide about the wedding?"

"Tell me,"

There is the when, where, who are attendants, and plans for the reception," she said in one breath.

"Oh, is that all? That can be done in a few minutes." Doug kissed her on the forehead when she didn't laugh.

"I'm serious but I know you're a kidder. Let's promise each other that we will have fun doing this."

"I promise." He hoped he could keep that promise.

*****

The trip home seemed shorter than the one to Masonberg. Teresa found it difficult to keep her mind on the road. Her thoughts kept returning to the unbelievable story of her parents and her birth. The man she had thought was her father was really her uncle! Why should she believe this old man she had never seen?

"Are you asleep, Jimbo?"

"No ma'am. Do you want to talk?"

Without answering him she began to talk.

"Why did it take all these years for someone to tell the secret? How could the maniac of a woman in that shack be my half sister? No way. I have to take some time off and go back to Masonberg and find the truth. The story I just heard could not be true. It was not possible. It sounded more like a fantasy novel. Had Lily's mother known any of this wild story? Lily, I haven't thought of her for days except when the old man mentioned my Dad's other wife and baby. If this wild tale is true then my hero, or the man I thought was my dad, gave up his life for me. Oh my God! He did love me more than Lily. But this tale couldn't be true. I will find out. I can't live like this the rest of my life.

Suddenly something loomed in her headlights. Hitting the brakes, the car lurched and Jimbo came part way into the front seat.

"Wow! What happened?"

"Something came out in the road but I stopped in time. I think it was a baby deer. I feel weak in the knees. Let's stop and eat that lunch you stole from the store." She smiled to herself. Now she was glad he did it.

"I'll have you know I didn't steal that lunch. It was part of my wages for working this morning."

"Jimbo, I'm not criticizing…..you deserved all you got. Let's drop the subject and enjoy the food."

Teresa found a shady spot under a large maple tree. She pulled off the road and turned off the engine. She looked at Jimbo, and asked him if he believed the old man's story. She was not expecting his answer.

"I have no background as you do, but I think part of it is true. I can't buy the part about your mama and the man you called daddy being twins. You're going back and find out the truth, ain't you, Teresa?

"Probably. Now where is that special lunch?" They both burst into laughter.

*****

Doug felt as if he were walking on clouds this special day. He didn't remember the trip from Lily's apartment to the store. The morning went fast as he waited on the steady stream of customers. Mr. Snead, the owner, was putting on his jacket to head out the door for his usual lunch at the

87

nearby diner. Doug looked at the clock as if he were seeing things. He couldn't believe half the day was gone.

"Hey Doug, what's up with you today? You look like that cat who swallowed the canary." Sylvia Wilson was Mr. Snead's secretary and right hand girl. He had heard rumors about their being too friendly but he chalked it up as just gossip. Sylvia was attractive but not a person who caused men's heads to turn. She had always acted like a lady around him.

"Well, I didn't have a canary for breakfast. Can't a fellow be happy without there being a reason?"

"No. There is always a reason and it's usually a woman. Am I right, Doug?"

"I will not tell a lie. I have to tell somebody. Lily and I are getting back together. Can you believe that? After all this time."

"Wow! That's great. Have you set a date yet?"

"As a matter of fact we are going to do that this evening. The sooner the better but I think Lily wants a big wedding since we eloped the first time. I guess she deserves it because of all the stuff I put her through.

"I can't imagine you not treating a woman right. You have such a sweet disposition."

"That is now and that was then. I suppose I have grown up and relaxed. Boy, was I immature I think Lily believes that I have changed or we wouldn't be back together again. What do you think?"

"Sounds good to me. I wish my boyfriend would change like that. When he gets to drinking which is most of the time, he can be very pushy. Sometimes I'm afraid of him."

"You shouldn't stay with someone like that. He could hurt you one day.

"I know but there is nowhere for me to go to get away from him. Doug barely heard her last words.

"Got to go to lunch now. Say "hi" to Lily and tell her I' m expecting an invitation to the wedding."

"That, I'll do. He would never have thought of asking Sylvia to the wedding. Maybe they would. It would be Lily's decision.

*****

As the hospital came into sight, Lily felt as if she had been gone for months. Panic set in as she tried to remember the new nurse's name who would be giving meds. What was the combination to the narcotic cabinet? She hurried through the front door and to the elevators.

"Lily, snap out of it! You are not a student any longer. You are a registered nurse with a responsible job. You are a good nurse.

The elevator door opened and she saw a nurse at the desk.

"Miss Ritter," good morning." The combination of the narcotic cabinet popped into her head. Lily you are back. She was fine.

She heard the swish of her uniform before she saw her. The Superintendent of Nurses had a way of being at your elbow before you knew she was around.

"Mrs. Lawson, it's great to see you. How's that sweet baby of yours?"

"She has grown so tall lately, I don't consider her a baby anymore. She seems to outgrow her clothes overnight."

Miss Hull had never married. Lily wondered how much she did know about babies. She seemed to care for Lily and had been extremely warm and outgoing this morning. What did she want Lily to do? Work extra for someone?

"Mrs. Lawson, when you get a few minutes, I need to talk to you. Come to my office. I'll see you shortly." Her starched uniform made a rustling sound as she turned and walked away.

Lily's heart was pounding in her temples. What have I done? Maybe I've been absent too long. Did I make a huge mistake with a patient? I've got to go and find out. A student nurse was standing at the desk waiting to ask her a question.

"May I help you, Miss Lang?" Name tags were certainly valuable.

"Not really, I just wanted to listen and maybe pick up a few things from you." She appeared unsure of her purpose. Lily remembered those early days of training.

"Well, you could be of tremendous help if you would stay at the desk, answer the phone and help anyone who walks up. I hope I won't be gone long. If you need help, Miss Nelson is giving meds.

"I'll be okay." She didn't sound too certain about that.

Miss Hull's door was open but Lily knocked out of courtesy.

"Come in, Mrs. Lawson. Have a seat. She motioned toward a straight backed wooden chair placed in front of her imposing, bare desk.

"I know you're wondering why I asked you to see me today. No, you haven't done anything wrong. As a matter of fact I want to offer you a supervisory position. Do you think you can handle the newborn nursery?"

Lily was floored. And speechless.

"I know you can do it. Did you enjoy your time in there when you were in training?"

"Yes, very much. I had thought of specializing in pediatric nursing."

"Mrs. Hancock has decided to take time off and have a little one of her own. She wants to leave in two weeks. She is fortunate. She has a husband who can support her." Miss Hull knew she had said the wrong thing.

I wonder if I should tell her. She will have to know soon.

"Miss Hull. Before you go on, I have some news. Doug and I are remarrying in a few weeks."

It took the nursing supervisor a few seconds to process the information.

"That's quite a surprise but I will leave that to your judgment. You're a sensible young woman and I know you will do the right thing. Could you make the wedding in two weeks and then take a week for a honeymoon? I don't think I can hold Mrs. Hancock any longer."

"I don't think we can have the wedding I've dreamed about all my life but I think we can work something out. Doug and I will make our plans tonight." She felt her hand tremble and she put it to her side.

"May I expect an answer tomorrow?"

"Yes." Lily forgot to say the superintendent's name as she turned and left the office

CHAPTER FOURTEEN

"Jimbo, are you going to sleep all day? Don't you remember what I told you last night? We have work to do before I take you home. By the way you have never explained to me about your family and where you live. Don't they care that you're away from home? Are you listening to me?"

He came down the stairs rubbing the sleep from his eyes.

"Coffee? I need coffee."

"It's on the counter. Do you want eggs or cereal?" She followed him into the kitchen.

"As good as your eggs are, cereal is fine. It's too hot to cook."

"You're so right."

"I have a lot of plans for today and I need your help. Are you with me?" She placed the cereal bowl down in front of him, just a little too hard.

"Hey, girl, are you mad at me?" I couldn't have done anything in my sleep. Or did I? Some people say I snore. Is that it?" That one -sided smile lit up his face.

"What are you so happy about, if I may ask?" She tried to imagine what could have changed his disposition so drastically from yesterday.

Teresa hadn't given much thought to his good humor in the past few days. She was concentrating on ending this Will charade and all the time wondering what her father really meant by the letter and its instructions.

"Oh, I'm just happy to have a bed and a roof over my head and a good breakfast. That's all. I don't want to talk about my family."

"So, I'm just a meal ticket?" Her tone was not one of humor.

"Don't be so touchy. I think you're a lot more than a meal ticket I like being around you because I never know what you'll do next." Staring into the bowl of cereal his thoughts went to the family he didn't want to talk about. There was only one person left and that was his father. At least he called himself his father. Sometimes Jimbo didn't believe he was the one. He didn't count his crazy grandfather anymore.

"Enough of this. We have a busy day ahead. We're going back to Masonberg but this time we're going prepared. After you finish your breakfast come up in the attic and help me look for something else that would give us my Dad's relationship with folks in that area."

"Be there in a minute."

*****

Although it was early morning, the attic was steamy hot. Teresa felt shaky and wanted this to be over soon. There was a large box way back in the corner. She had to move several others, crumbling cartons with some effort. As she lifted the last, one its bottom came out and the contents spilled over the attic floor. She started to say something that in the past would have resulted in her mother washing out her mouth with lye soap. That was years ago but the stinging taste had remained with her.

94

As she began to pick up the contents from the carton of old receipts and bills, her hand hit against something firm. Digging around she uncovered a small square object which appeared to be a receipt book or maybe a diary. With trembling hands she opened it to the first page. Immediately her eyes fell upon the top line and she knew she had found the treasure. "The Last Will and Testament of Frank Jacob Fain." Her father was so clever. He knew she wouldn't bother to look in a box of old receipts. She couldn't believe her good fortune.

She forgot the steamy heat of the attic and settled down with her back against a two by four stud. Teresa was just a paragraph into the reading when she knew this was not a legal document. It had the legal language of a last will and testament but it read more like a story or a confession. Her father was telling the strange family secret of his sister's illegitimate child and the whole sordid story that had been embellished by the neighbors and family members. She couldn't stop reading.

Dear Teresa,

If you're the one reading this you have no doubt been told the truth about your lineage. I wish it could have been different for you, but some things we have no control over. I would have given my life so that your mother could have lived and been a good mother to you,

I'm so sorry I had to lie to you over the years but I did it with love in my heart. I always had the feeling you thought I loved Lily more than you. I love both of you with every cell in my body. I felt I had to do what I did for my sister, your mother.

I didn't tell Anna the truth and we all suffered for it. I pray that you don't hate me. That would be more than I could bear. Please remember why I did what I did and try to make Lily understand.

If you're reading this letter you must have accomplished all the items on the list I left you. Now it is time for you to find the inheritance I have left to my family. I wish it could be more but please use your share wisely and you will have a comfortable life.

By now you probably know my attorney's name. You should make an appointment with him and he will tell you of your's and Lily's inheritance.

Love,
Dad

Teresa's heart beat a little faster. No, she didn't know the attorney's name because Mr. Mason was dead and she couldn't talk to him. Someone else must know. She quickly closed the box and hurried down the shaky attic stairs.

"Jimbo, where are you?" No answer. He had decided he wanted no part of the attic after feeling the heat coming down from the opening.

Again, "Jimbo, I need you."

He heard her this time and came running.

"Yes, what is it big sister? She wasn't certain she liked that title. She was not his sister. She was no one's sister, not even Lily's. They didn't have the same father or mother. That was that. She didn't see why she must share the inheritance with her. She had to find a way to keep it all.

But first she must find her father's lawyer. Then the thought hit her. There weren't that many in the whole town, she didn't think. Going to the desk, she picked up the phone book and started to look though the attorney's names. Maybe she would see one that rang a bell with her.

Teresa was almost to the end of the list, nothing looked familiar. Then she saw it--Jubal Joyce--a name to remember. She had dialed his number before she had any doubts that this was the person.

"Attorney Joyce's office," a cracked voice said. Teresa could picture an old lady old enough to be Attorney Joyce's mother.

"My name is Teresa (she didn't say her last name because at times she forgot who she lied to about her name being Taylor). She had never liked the name Fain and couldn't wait to change it) and I believe Mr. Joyce was my father's attorney. His name was Frank Fain."

"Yes, Miss Fain, he has been awaiting your call. Would you like to come in this afternoon about 3:00? The voice sounded stronger now.

"Yes, I could make that."

As she hung up the phone she wondered why Mr. Joyce was expecting her just now.

*****

Lily had the day off and Doug told her to sleep late. He would watch Anna Rose until it was time for her to go shopping with Sarah, on the search for a special wedding dress. The wedding date seemed to be coming faster than they could ever have imagined.

Lily had been restless all night, tossing and turning, dreaming about her wedding plans.

She awoke the next morning still feeling as if she were in the dream. The ringing of the telephone brought her into reality.

"Hello, this is Lily."

"Hi, sweetheart. Did you finally get some rest? I worry about you."

"I'm fine but let me tell you about the strangest dream I had. Do you have time?"

"Well, if it's not more than an hour long!" He laughed.

"I'll hurry." And this is what she told her husband to be:

LILY'S DREAM

I had been awake for some time, planning and thinking about our upcoming wedding. I would start to enter that hazy phase before sleep and it would be Tom instead of you standing at the altar waiting for me. Don't be upset Doug, it was just a dream. No response.

Exhaustion took over and I fell into a deep sleep. I remembered the wedding dress in every detail. Or was that Rose's dress? I felt so confused. Was I doing the right thing? Was Doug for real? Would he stay this way---an attentive husband and good father to his daughter?

Slowly I began to ascend up into the night sky. The stars were bright and the moon full. As I looked down, houses, streets, cars and trees were visible in the moonlight.

In a flash I was over the little chapel of St Andrews near Bittersweet, Rose's girlhood home. The lights were on and I descended just enough to see in a window near the chancel area. There stood Father Jackson, Tom and someone beside him I couldn't quite make out. On the other side was Rose, how beautiful she looked! And there was Sarah and Anna Rose with a basket of rose petals in her hands. I floated around to another window. Sitting straight and tall in rows like statues on the worn pews were Aunt Margaret, James, Abe, Andy, and yes, there was Doug sitting stone faced beside him. I didn't know what to do and suddenly the tears came gushing out and made two ribbons quickly joining and becoming a stream as they fell to the ground. I began to fall and soon I was sinking into the stream of tears. I felt a sense of peace although I knew I must be drowning. Suddenly I took a deep breath and awoke in my own bed.

"Doug. What do you make of that?" He hadn't said a word and she was regretting telling him the dream.

She peeked to see if he had fallen asleep. He looked as if he had eaten a sour apple. Then he let out the biggest belly laugh she had ever heard.

"Lily, it was just a dream. I know you've been through a lot in the past few years but life is going to be better. I promise."

She couldn't believe this man. Was he the same Doug she had married as a young girl just out of high school? Then she remembered she wasn't that same girl. They both had changed and she knew this time their marriage would work.

CHAPTER FIFTEEN

Teresa was surprised when she located Attorney Joyce's office. Pulling up in front of the old run down house she knew she had made a mistake. She took the piece of paper from her purse just to double check. Yes, the sign said, 1800 Locust Street. Strange!

As she opened the large door, which needed a coat of paint, she heard singing from within. A clear, melodic soprano was practicing the scales with perfect pitch.

"Excuse me, I'm looking for Attorney Joyce." Her eyes met those of a heavy set lady seated at a desk at the front of a large reception room. A few chairs and a couple of love seats were placed sparsely throughout the room.

"You must be Miss Teresa Fain." Her voice was surprisingly soft after the notes still lingering in the air.

"Yes, that's me."

"Have a seat and I'll tell Mr. Joyce you are here."

In about five minutes the office door opened and there stood the most handsome man Teresa had ever seen. He was tall and slender with cold black hair with just a little natural curl, giving him a boyish look. His deep blue eyes were an oddity with his complexion and dark hair. His expensive silk suit fit him perfectly. Teresa felt her heart skip a beat.

"Good afternoon, Teresa. May I call you, Teresa?"

She couldn't make her mouth say "yes" so she just nodded.

"Step into my office. We have a few things to talk about." He touched her very lightly on the shoulder as she walked past him through the door. Teresa felt something like an electrical charge quickly pass her body.

"I expected you a few days ago. Your Dad told me how quick and smart you are. I don't mean to imply that you aren't."

"Well, I don't quite know how to answer that. I've had some disturbing things happen since I started on the search for my father's Will. John Mason, the man who was supposed to tell me everything, is dead. I didn't know where to turn but I kept on looking until I found it in the strangest place. She smiled at him. He didn't smile back but she could see the humor in his eyes.

"Do you have a safe place to stay? How are you traveling back and forth to Masonberg? Do you go alone?

"I did the first time but a young man who is from that area returned with me and went back the second time. Actually he was the one who helped me find Mr. Mason . His name is Jimbo and he is full of information. He has been a big help.

"I'm sure he has, but be wary of young men being too helpful when money is involved." He looked at her as if she had already done something wrong.

"I think he is okay. So far he hasn't been told that there might be a large sum of money left.

"Teresa, do you have the letter your father left you? I had my doubts about your ever finding it! But your father said he knew you and that you were a clever girl. I think he was right."

"I hope he was".

As she handed him the crumpled letter, his hand touched hers. He smiled slightly. She couldn't take her eyes off him as he strode to a file cabinet near his desk, moving as easily and quickly as a well trained athlete. His tailored, silk suit seemed a part of his skin. He turned toward her and she quickly averted her eyes toward the floor. But he noticed.

"Teresa, I have your Father's Will here in this folder. Am I right in assuming that your mother has passed away?"

"Yes, I'm sorry to say that she has." Despite her last troubled years, Teresa found herself wishing she had her Mother to talk to about what was going on now.

"Have you been in contact recently with your half-sister, Lily?"

She had planned to lie to him but she couldn't. She blurted out, "No, I have not tried to contact her recently. I hear that she is planning a wedding."

"That's interesting. Anyone you know?"

"Yes, yes, it's her former husband, Doug. I think it's a wrong move on her part."

"What about his part?" He could hear the resentment in her voice.

"I don't know about him except that he doesn't appear to be the marrying kind. It didn't work the first time."

"Well, since Lily is one of the heirs in this Will, I'm afraid it cannot be read without her being present." He saw the look of disgust on her face.

"Lily didn't go through this stupid treasure hunt to earn the right to hear the Will. Why does she have to be here?"

"Because that is the law. And your father would want it that way. So will you contact her or shall I?"

"You do it. She doesn't pay attention to what I say anyway." She looked as if she were pouting.

"I will call her today if her current number is in the folder."

"She works at the hospital. I bet she's there now."

"Thank you, I will try there first. Would you mind stepping out into the waiting room while I talk to her?"

She started to say that she did mind and what did he have to say to Lily that he couldn't say in front of her? But she held her tongue and walked into the waiting room and sat down.

The time seemed to drag by. Teresa picked up a magazine from the end table and began flipping though worn pages. What is taking so long? Maybe she is not at work today.

Then the door to the attorney's office opened.

"Teresa, please come back in. He held the door for her. As she brushed past him she smelled his expensive cologne.

The first words out of his mouth were, "Lily seems like such a nice girl. You don't agree do you? Have you tried to have a conversation with her?"

Teresa wanted to tell Mr. Smarty Pants how she felt about Lily but she held her tongue. There was no need to make him angry with her. She liked him too much.

He came closer and looked her in the eye.

"Teresa, I want you to make me a promise. Offer to go and pick up Lily and bring her here tomorrow afternoon at 2:00. It happens to be her day off. We will have the reading of the Will at that time. Are we on the same page?" His eyes were looking at her as if he could see through her.

"Yes, I will do that." She turned and walked out the door. She knew if she stayed her mouth would get her in trouble

*****

She felt as if she were on a treadmill, going nowhere. Lily didn't have a clue how much work a small wedding required. She and Doug had eloped on a whim the first time around. Now she wanted things to be done right. How she wished her mother were still living. She relished in making lists and doing all the nitty gritty things that would result in a fantastic wedding. She hadn't realized how much she missed her until now. She needed some help. Rose, no, she was too busy. Aunt Margaret. Why hadn't she thought of her before?

She almost skipped to the phone. Dialing a number she had known for years, she anxiously awaited an answer.

"Hello, came through in a weak voice. Lily wasn't sure it was Aunt Margaret.

"Aunt Margaret, is that you? This is Lily."

"Oh, Lily how good to hear your voice. What's this I hear about you getting married? The young man, whoever he is, is a lucky one." Her voice had become a little stronger.

"It's Doug, Aunt Margaret. We've decided that we can make a go of it this time. We have both matured. And Anna Rose needs both parents."

"I'm so happy for you, Lily. When is the big day?"

"Well, that's kind of why I'm calling. I realize that even a small wedding takes a lot of planning and work. Could you help me, Aunt Margaret?"

"I'll be glad to do what I can. My health is not good anymore." She began to cough uncontrollably.

"I wouldn't ask you to do anything physical. I just need your support and advice. You probably still remember some of the things Rose did for her wedding.

"Or even mine," she said with a chuckle.

Oh, I'm sorry, Aunt Margaret. You had such a beautiful wedding. I remember it was Spring and the dogwoods were in bloom. You were a beautiful bride."

"Thank you my dear. Everyone, including you, helped to make it very special." She began to cough again.

If you say, yes, you'll help me, I'll pick you up this Saturday morning and take you to the Bridal shop. You'll just have to sit and offer your opinions. That shouldn't get too hard, should it?"

"I think I can handle that. I'm so excited for you Lily. You deserve a beautiful wedding. How's that sweet little girl of yours?"

"She is well and happy. I can't believe I've been blessed with such a good child."

"Well she takes after her mother. You were a quiet little thing. Sometimes I worried about you."

"I was fine . They say my Daddy was a quiet person."

"I didn't know him but I'm sure he was a fine person. What time will you pick me up on Saturday?"

How about 10:00? Most of the stores don't open until 10:00 anyway."

"See you then." Lily wished she could have talked longer.

*****

I cannot believe I'm here. What number did she say? I'm getting too soft. I'm feeling good about seeing Lily. What am I going to say? I had this big plan to keep her from inheriting any of my father's estate and now it's like a fading dream. It will come back. It has to or I might as well go in there, take her hand and drag her to the lawyer's office and give her half the money. I won't do it. She doesn't deserve any of it. Here I am. I don't think I can do this. What has come over me. If I believed in such things I would think my dad was controlling me from the grave.

Teresa pushed the bell. She hoped no one was home.

"Teresa, it's been a long time. Come in. To what do I owe this pleasure?"

How sickening. I'll keep smiling but I'll make this short and sweet.

"I came to tell you that our father's Will is going to be read tomorrow afternoon. Can you make it? Of course if you cannot, we'll understand." What a lie, Teresa.

Tomorrow afternoon? I think I can. I heard you mention something about it being misplaced. I take it that you found it."

"Yes, it was in the attic all the time, I just didn't look hard enough. Our dad had quite a sense of humor. Did you know that?

"Well, I wasn't around him all that much when I was old enough to remember. My mother told me some things

107

about him and I think she did mention his sense of humor. Are there some funny things in the Will?" She couldn't imagine that.

"No, not in the Will, just what I had to do to find it." She would not go into all that with Lily.

"I'll see you tomorrow afternoon at Attorney Joyce's office. Here is the address on this slip of paper." She started toward the door.

"Teresa, wouldn't you like to see your niece?"

"Niece? Oh, you mean your little girl? Is she taking a nap?"

"Yes, but it's about time for her to wake up. I'll get her."

"No, don't wake her. I must go and she needs her rest.

She hurried out the apartment door.

Lily stood there staring at the door and wondering what her problem was.

The ringing of the phone brought Lily out of her daze.

"Hello," At first she didn't hear the faint voice.

"Speak up. I can't hear you." Then she realized it was Rose.

"Lily, this is Rose. Something terrible has happened." She began to sob.

"Rose, you're scaring me. What is it?" She felt the energy drain from her body and reached for the side of the bed.

"It's Aunt Margaret"....and then Lily thought she heard the receiver hit something.

"Rose, are you there? Speak to me." Then she heard a scream like she had never heard in all her years of nursing. It couldn't have been Rose. That horrible guttural sound could not have come from petite Rose. And then a deafening silence. Nothing. Not even a crackle of the phone line.

"Someone please answer me. Please." Lily broke down in sobs because she knew. Aunt Margaret had died.

"Lily." A male voice came through. "This is Andy. I'm afraid Rose can't talk now. James found Aunt Margaret dead this morning when he got up. She was cold so she passed away hours before. Lily, can you come over? I don't know what to do for Rose and James. The doctor just left and I think James will be able to sleep awhile. I knew Margaret's death would be hard on Rose but I didn't expect her to be crushed this way. I want to fix her broken heart but I don't know where to start."

*****

The sweet, sickening smell of lilies and carnations brought back visions of her mother's funeral service. She felt the nausea rising higher. She must not think about it, Rose needed her to be strong. And James, she had never seen anyone more devastated by a loved one's death. Sarah called the doctor for fear he would die of a broken heart. He was going on tranquilizers and sheer will power today. He would not and could not swallow solid food. Everyone kept urging him to drink plenty of fluids. He looked as if he were caught in an endless nightmare.

Lily heard the organ playing Aunt Margaret's favorite hymns. She saw the people pouring into the little Episcopal Church. She had never let her mind think of this day. Certain people come into your life and you think of them being there always. Aunt Margaret was one of those. I never thought about her not being here forever. She would leave a large void in so many people's lives.

Rose squeezed her hand and the two best friends looked at one another and smiled ever so faintly. The thought ran through Lily's mind that she must make a concentrated effort to see her best friend more often.

CHAPTER SIXTEEN

"What a beautiful service! She'll be missed. She lived such a good life. Poor James. I hope he can make it without her. I never saw anyone grieve as hard as Rose. I wonder what will become of Bittersweet." These were just some of the things Lily remembered overhearing after the service in the cemetery. Did people think she was deaf?" No. they just didn't think. She felt more alone than she had in all her life. It shouldn't be this way. Doug was here beside her. They would be married in a few days...right here in this little church where there was so much sadness today. Would she feel happier on her wedding day? Oh, Aunt Margaret, I never knew how much you meant to me. To think I called you two days ago and asked for your help. It had been months since I called. What must you think of me or thought of me? You can't know what I'm thinking now. Or maybe you can. I don't know about such things. Is there life after death? I've been a doubter all my life. If someone could give me proof that God really exists and there is a heaven, I would believe and take Anna Rose to church. I hope she can believe the Bible stories. Even as a small child I found them much like fairy tales. Aunt Margaret would be ashamed of me.... she lived her faith every day.

"Doug, do you mind if I go and spend time with Rose? I know she must be hurting so much." Lily saw his smile and knew it was okay. Letting go of his hand, she hurried across the parking lot to where Rose was standing with family members. She recognized several cousins from Kingsport and Johnston City.

"Rose, do you mind if I stay with you for awhile. I feel we need each other now. I've missed you." She reached for Rose's hand.

"I'm so glad you came over. Just thinking about Aunt Margaret makes me think of you. We wouldn't need to talk. We seem to read one another's mind." And she smiled

"Is anyone living in the little house now? "She was hoping she and her friend could go to the attic room and look out over the Estate of Bittersweet.

"I think the renters moved out about a month ago. Come on. We'll have to open the windows to let in the fresh air."

Both girls almost skipped as they headed for Rose's car that would take them to the little white cottage next to the big house.

*****

Seeing Rose and Lily leave the parking lot of the church, Teresa felt an overwhelming pang of jealousy.

"Why does it matter to me? I can take care of myself. They need other people to get them out of trouble. Stupid Lily can't even keep a husband. I won't let her have half of my Daddy's money. She felt the jealously and envy crawl up her spine. Why did she care? Things would change tomorrow. Somehow she would get Lily's share of the inheritance. She hadn't thought of a way to keep Lily from getting her half of the money. She wouldn't give up. Even after the Will was probated she could keep trying. She started for home and another restless night.

Across town Attorney Joyce was beside himself with anger and bewilderment. He paced from one end of the office to the other. Back and forth. His secretary had never seen him in such a state. Around the courthouse he was known as, Mr. Cool."

He opened his office door so he could use her as a sounding board.

"What happened to the money? Where had the receipts gone? Who could have tricked the bank? I know it was not Teresa She is unaware of where it has been all these years. Did everyone think there was more money than was truly in the account?" So many questions. First, I need to find someone in Masonberg. John Mason is dead and he is the one who knows everything about this convoluted mess. I should have been more aware of what was transpiring but I thought it was all an innocent game. I dread to tell Teresa. She has expected to inherit a large sum of money all along. I wonder if the game her Father had her to participate in has given her a different outlook on life."

*****

"Hello, Lily. This is Teresa. I was sorry to hear about Aunt Margaret. Such a shock." There was only silence on the other end of the phone.

Finally, "Thank you, Teresa. It has been such a loss for all of us, especially Rose and James."

113

"Would you like me to pick you up tomorrow ? I would be glad to. (Just a little lie). There's something I need to run by you."

"What time?"

"I'll be there about 1:00. That will give us some extra time to talk."

"See you then. Bye."

The receiver clicked. "It will be my pleasure, sister, dear."

*****

The striking clock echoed throughout the empty house. Its sound seemed to hang in the stillness of the silent house. James was aware of the chimes but they didn't mean anything but noise. If Margaret were here he would have counted the strikes and known it was time to start supper. It didn't matter today. He was not hungry and felt he would never want to eat again. The only feeling he had was numbness and that was like having no feeling. Margaret was his life, his spirit, his soul. Now she was no more and he might as well have died with her. It was an effort for him just to take a breath. It was only three days ago when he awaked and his sweet Margaret had not. Did she call to him? Did she awake with pain? Maybe he could have done something to help. Hadn't he in the past? He remembered the time during a blizzard when a fire truck plowed through snow drifts encrusted in ice to rescue her and take her to the hospital.

"James, it's Rose. I brought some supper." She didn't feel so cheery but something had to be done to bring James back to reality. She was afraid he would stop eating and become ill.

"I'm here, Rose. I don't think I can eat. I'm just not hungry."

"Well, just come and sit with me. I have your favorite soup. Maybe you'll change your mind." She took the basket to the kitchen and began to set the food on the counter. James followed with slow steps and hunched shoulders.

"Is Sarah keeping the baby?"

Rose could barely hear his soft voice, He looked completely exhausted.

"Yes, I thought it better if he stay there and go to bed early. It was a long day and he was getting cranky.

"Please bring him over tomorrow, Rose." The words came out as little flutters.

"James, let me help you prepare for bed. I can put my nursing skills to work."

Just a faint smile and he nodded as if he was too exhausted to speak. Rose reached out for his hand and he began to walk toward her very slowly. She was thankful they had an elevator.

CHAPTER SEVENTEEN

"Right on time, Teresa." Lily had been trying to guess what her half-sister wanted to talk about. She had a feeling that it wasn't good.

"I always try to be on time. Nothing bothers me anymore than someone showing up late." She seemed to be agitated about something.

"Teresa, don't keep me waiting. Just tell me what you want to talk to me about."

"Well, I've wanted to have this talk for a long time but just couldn't bring myself to do it. But the time has come. You know that today we will be hearing our father's Will read. What do you think it will say? I have an idea. Do you?"

Lily was beginning to think that this free ride to the attorney's was not going to be pleasant. She felt as if she were being held captive by her agitated half-sister.

"I haven't given it much thought. I've been busy with other things and now with Aunt Margaret's death my mind has not been on my father's Will."

"Well, I guess I'm glad to hear that. Then this Will is not a big deal to you? Is that what I'm hearing?" Her voice had an edge to it that Lily didn't like.

"I guess that's what I'm saying. I've never given much thought to my father having a great deal to leave his family. Is there something I don't know?"

"Well, you could say that. He invented something for the mining industry and I understand the rights on that special tool has amounted to a lot. I'm glad you didn't know about this and I guess you might be more agreeable to what I'm going to ask you." She had a devious tone to her voice. Lily was beginning to get anxious.

"What do you want me to agree to, Teresa? Tell me and maybe I will." Her hands began to shake.

"Maybe you will? Since you never lived with our father for very long I would say that you and he were not very close. Right? I mean we lived together until his death little more than a year ago. We couldn't have been closer, except for one thing….he loved you more than he loved me."

"How do you know that? He didn't abandon you. You had him all those years…I didn't and my Mother never got over his leaving." She tried to hold back the tears.

"I don't understand why, Lily. I just know he did. He wanted me to be just like you. He didn't have to say it. I knew."

"Please get to the point and tell me what you want. You're making me very nervous."

"Well, well. So you can lose your cool? I thought nurses were calm and cool at all times."

"We're not usually threatened personally."

"Threatened! I haven't threatened you, Lily. I just want to ask you to do one thing for me. Okay, here goes. Since you have an education and will soon marry or should I say, remarry your husband and both of you have good jobs and you have that rich friend, Rose, why can't you let me have all of my Father's estate? There, I said it. Now what do you say?"

"My question is why should I do that? He was my father, too? If my Mother was still living, I believe she would tell me to refuse your request."

"But your mother is dead and our father is dead and we are in his Will. I want all of the money to make up for his not loving me the way he loved you."

"Do you think money can make up for someone not loving you? I think I'm beginning to feel sorry for you, maybe just a little.

"I don't want your sympathy! I want your part of the inheritance. Are you going to give it to me or will I have to take it?" She stopped the car and turned to glare at Lily.

Lily was suddenly aware that they had left the city limits. She was beginning to realize how aggressive Teresa could be and she was uneasy.

"Teresa, where are we going? The lawyer's office is not out here in the country."

"I want your answer. Now. Will you give me your part of the inheritance?"

Lily couldn't believe Teresa's words. She had known her half-sister was different but she had no idea how selfish she was.

"How could I keep the money knowing how you feel? You can have my share."

"You're something else, Lily. You're too good to be true. Now if you make me eat my words, you will be sorry. Since our father is dead I don't have any one to answer to."

"If I give you my word it is good as a contract. My Mother told me that I got the honesty gene from her grandfather. I don't know about that but I've always felt better inside if I told the whole truth." She couldn't determine if the expression on Teresa's face was one of shock or disgust.

"You'll have to make a believer out of me. Here is what I want you to say to the hot shot lawyer." She handed Lily a piece of paper torn from a tablet that appeared to be old.

"Sorry I couldn't find any fine stationery for my "better than thou" half-sister. The message is the same. Read it to me ... with feeling."

Lily knew she would try to do whatever Teresa told her to do, within reason. She had to squint in the dim light of the car.

"My name is Lily Lawson and I am Teresa's half sister. I did not know my father except what my mother told me about him. Since he left her and me when I was a baby she didn't say a lot of positive things. I don't feel a closeness or love for a parent as I should. Therefore, I am refusing my part of the inheritance. My half-sister, Teresa, is entitled to all of it."

"That was fair but you can put more feeling into it. Read it again."

CHAPTER EIGHTEEN

She couldn't shake the uneasy feeling she had this morning. It was not the deep sadness she felt about Aunt Margaret. This was something to do with the living. Rose was not normally a worrier but she couldn't shake this depressive sense of doom. She said nothing to Andy about it. He was so concerned about her wellbeing that she didn't want him to worry even more. Lily was on her mind, too. She had been terribly shaken over Aunt Margaret's death. At first Rose was a little surprised but after some thought she realized that Aunt Margaret was like a second mother to Lily. She hadn't been aware of the closeness until after her Aunt's death.

Her mind wandered back to the day she arrived at the bus station in Bristol. She was only twelve years old and she had suddenly become an orphan.

She recalled the bus pulling into the bus station in Bristol. She could still hear the bus driver................

"Bristol, Virginia on one side of the street and Bristol, Tennessee on the other."

As she slowly stepped down from the bus, Rose looked for a fair skinned lady who might be searching for a little lost girl. She didn't see anyone who fit the description.

"Little Lady, here is your suitcase," called out the bus driver. "Is someone meeting you?"

She nodded and tried to smile to give an air of confidence, but the dried tears made her cheeks feel stiff. She turned and walked into the terminal. Maybe Aunt Margaret was in there. She was sure that must be it--she

121

probably needed to sit down and rest. The place was filled with smoke; a country song was blaring from the juke box. A few scarred wooden benches were sitting in the middle of the floor. An old man in tattered overalls was asleep in the corner of one. The others were empty , except for a lone gray haired lady frantically going through a well worn purse. There was something about her profile that drew Rose a little closer. Suddenly, the woman raised her head and made eye contact with Rose. "Rose! Is that you, Rose?"She suddenly got up and walked closer.

"Is that you, Aunt Margaret? You don't look like I thought you would. I thought you would be….."And her voice trailed off. A faint smile crinkled the wrinkles at the corner of her mouth. You thought I would look younger and I thought you would look older!" They both laughed.

What a good memory! That was the first day of my new and wonderful life. Thank you, Aunt Margaret.

She hadn't realized she had been crying until she felt the tears trickle down her cheeks and fall gently into her lap.

Suddenly the thought of James gave her a start. She knew he was hurting more than he would admit. He was an honest, truly good man. Aunt Margaret had known that all along, and she let him know how she felt. Their's was the best love story she knew.

The very first time she was introduced to Mr. James Robinson was at John Keller's funeral. James was Mr. Keller's butler, chauffeur, and secretary. When Aunt Margaret introduced them, James offered her his hand and bowed slightly. She knew he was a gentleman and a kind man just from that one gesture

It was soon after that when Aunt Margaret asked Mr. Robinson to have supper with them in the tiny house.

"I thought we could invite him over for supper tonight. He is all alone in that house, and I know he would like some company. I never liked to eat alone. How about you?"

"Me neither. Do you think you could make some of your vegetable soup and some cornbread?"

"Don't you think we could do better than that for company? What about some fried chicken?" Margaret smiled in spite of herself. She thought Rose was fond of her soup because she was so hungry the first evening she arrived.

I asked Aunt Margaret how I could help her make supper. She probably suspected I didn't know a lot about cooking. She sent me outside to gather some holly bows for the table. James commented on them later, how they added to the festive table. Although he was a quiet man, he was known for complimenting others. I don't remember a lot about the supper except that I was smitten with James. I had never known a man who was as gentle and kind. I think I had a crush on him for years.

*****

"That was much better, Lily. I think we're ready to go to the lawyer's office. We have a few minutes before we get there. You can spend that time memorizing the words. I want it to sound as if it's coming straight from your heart." She turned the key and the car moved out onto the highway.

"Teresa?"

"You should be memorizing the words." Teresa's voice carried a sharp edge.

"I wish I knew why you feel the way you do about me. I would try to make it right, if I could."

"Don't ask me that again. You can't fix the way I feel. It's been that way since I knew you were in the world." Her words cut like sharp knife.

"I won't ask again, Teresa. I feel sorry for you." said so quietly that Teresa was unsure of the words. Lily began to cry softly.

Teresa pulled into the parking lot at the office of Attorney Joyce. Lily sat there frozen as if a statue."

"Lily, you can get out now. Remember our little talk. Say the words I gave you and everything will be okay. Any questions?"

"No, Teresa. I think I know what you want. It really was never that important to me but I would have liked some money for Anna Rose's education." She started up the walk ahead of Teresa.

Lily's words hit a nerve. Was she denying Anna Rose an education? No, Teresa, that is Lily's responsibility, was the answer to herself.

Lily and Teresa walked into the lawyer's office at exactly 2:00 p.m.. The receptionist rose and ushered them right into Mr. Joyce's office. Her smile seemed fake.

"Good afternoon ladies".

CHAPTER NINETEEN

Doug Looked at his watch again. This afternoon seemed to be on slow time. Just as he was about to straighten things on the counter again, the bell over the door rang, Great! A customer.

"Hi, Abe. Boy. am I glad to see you. I think my watch has stopped."

"Getting anxious to get home to Lily?" There was a twinkle in his eyes that matched his smile.

"You know me too well, my friend. But I guess I'm a little worried about Lily being with Teresa today. Teresa was to pick her up and take her for the reading of their father's Will."

"Sounds pretty harmless to me. How about Anna Rose?"

"Anna Rose was fine when I came by Lily's this morning. Lily was excited about going to the attorney's office with Teresa. Come to think of it, she was more concerned than excited about what Teresa wanted to talk about. Maybe that is what is concerning me. I have never trusted Teresa completely. There was just something that always seemed phony about her. I hope I'm wrong. Oh, I'll try to forget it. I'm becoming a worry wart since Lily and I got back together I'm still in shock over her decision. I suppose I'm afraid something will go wrong. My Mother has always teased me about worrying about everything like an old woman. I will have to try and get over that after we're married. Married! What a great word. Just a few weeks and Lily and I will be married again.

"So how is it with you, my friend?" It was always good to see Abe. Doug had never understood why the older man had taken him under his wing after he and Lily were married the first time. Maybe he thought of him as a lonely young man who needed guidance. For whatever reason Abe had taken a liking to him, Doug could always count on his friendship. Abe brought memories of the summer after he and Lily divorced. It seemed to go on longer than the summers back home in the mountains. Doug missed his friends, Abe in particular. There was no one in Martinsburg to ask to go fishing. It really wasn't the matter of catching a fish but the camaraderie of a male friend he missed.

"Oh, pretty good. I came over ot see if my fishing buddy could spare a couple hours this Saturday to fish and talk."

"A couple hours, huh? When did we ever go fishing for a couple of hours?" Doug's laugh brought a smile to Abe's face.

"I guess three or four would be more like it."

Well, it just so happens that Lily and the girls are having one of those girls only get togethers and I'm free. Oh, maybe not. I think I'm supposed to keep Anna Rose."

"If I had to guess I would think Sarah would be delighted to take her to the girls thing and that way Lily can enloy being the guest of honor. How's that?"

Abe, it will probably work. Are you planning to give me the "before the wedding talk?" He chuckled.

"No, it's been so long since we had a long talk, I wanted to catch up."

"I'm looking forward to it my friend." He had thought about how unusual their friendship was considering the age difference.

"How about I pick you up Saturday morning about 7:00?"

"Okay. Bring some of that good coffee you're known for."

"Will do. Give Lily and the baby hugs from me."

Doug watched the old pickup until it was out of sight.

"What a nice man, he said out loud."

*****

"Mrs. Lawson, I am hearing you correctly? You want no part of your Father's estate? That is a true statement? Please answer, yes or no."

The look of surprise remained on his kind face. There was something not quite right here. Why would this single mother who has a job but not one that pays that well, refuse an inheritance? She couldn't possibly know that there is very little left. I cannot imagine what Miss Teresa Taylor will do when she hears. I dread this.

"Mr. Joyce, does that mean that all of my father's estate goes to me?" She was about to come up out of her chair. Mr. Joyce thought she might start dancing any moment.

"Yes, Miss Taylor, it looks that way. Would you like for me to read the Will now?" He wished he had at least given her a warning about what she was about to hear. He took the Will from a folder on his desk.

"Hmm, I, Frank Jacob Fain, being of sound mind, do bequeath.........(Teresa heard only the cadence of his voice until she thought he said "in the amount of $500.00).

"Five hundred dollars! Don't you mean five thousand dollars, at least?" She had lost all color in her face.

"Five hundred is correct. I have checked several times. It seems that someone improved the equipment your Father invented and his stock became a loser. I'm sorry but five hundred is all that is left." He was still waiting for the explosion.

"Don't you say a word, Lily. Why do you always seem to win? I hate you, Lily Lawson. Now I guess you and Doug will have this big wedding in a few days and will live happily ever after. And I will take my big fortune of $500.00 and live a "hand to mouth" life. It's not fair." She stormed out the door leaving Lily and Mr. Joyce with mouths agape.

"I'm sorry Mrs. Lawson. I will be more than glad to take you home."

"That's nice of you but I will see if one of my family members can come." She tried to smile at him but her mouth was so dry that she could not.

"If there is a problem, I will be honored to take you home. Maybe I shouldn't say this and I hope it doesn't embarrass you, but after what Teresa did to you, you should have been very upset."

"Mr. Joyce, I'm far from being a saint but I feel sorry for Teresa. She was right...I have had a better life than she."

"I admire you Mrs. Lawson. If you ever need a lawyer, please call."

"Thank you. I need to use your phone."

"Certainly, sit here at my desk. I'll be back shortly."

Lily dialed Abe's number and Sarah answered on the second ring.

"Sarah, would it be possible to come and get me at the lawyer's office" It's a long story and I'll tell you on the way home."

"I'll be there as soon as I can."

"Thanks, Sarah."

Lily sat back in the big leather chair and wished this had all been a dream. She truly felt sorry for Teresa but she wished she would leave and make a life elsewhere.

"Mrs. Lawson, I have something to give you."

She was startled and a little embarrassed that she was still in his chair.

"For me? Is it something to do with my father's will?"

"I believe it's a letter. I didn't open it. It's possible you will find answers to some of your questions in its contents. Whatever it contains I wish you the best of life's gifts. You've shown your giving spirit here today."

He handed her the envelope and quickly left the room.

Dear Lily,

Where do I begin? If you are reading this, you have heard the Will. I hope and pray that you received enough to make your life more comfortable. Maybe it will make up just a little for my not being there when you were a child. No matter what you have heard or read I always loved you and your Mother. If I had my life to live over, I would

have stayed with you two. Try to forgive me.
Your loving Dad,

CHAPTER TWENTY

It was a foggy morning. A humid silence fell over the lake where Abe and Doug sat quietly in a john boat. The two men, one old and one young, had talked all the way there. Now they were concentrating on the fish. Perhaps they were thinking about things to say on their way home.

Doug, the younger, had so much to think about. He would be married in six days. He had a long list given to him by Lily. He knew how much planning had gone into this wedding and he would see that every task on the list was done. He could not believe that Lily was giving him a second chance.

Abe's main reason for asking Doug was to run something by him and see his reaction. He knew it was asking a big favor but he and Sarah knew this was a new, more responsible Douglas Lawson. He felt certain that he was up to the task.

He knew from all the research and information from his doctor that his Parkinson's condition would worsen. His concern was for Sarah's welfare. He wanted Doug to consent to be in charge of her wellbeing when he could no longer care for himself. Remarrying Lily was the icing on the cake. Lily and Sarah had always been close.

"Hey, you got one, Doug! That's a big one."

Doug slowly played the bass in closer to the boat. As soon as it came into reach, he put the net under it. With a quick flick of his wrist he pulled the hook from the fish's wide mouth and freed it to live awhile longer.

"Douglas, why did you do that? You usually keep all the big ones."

"I'm feeling very generous today. Do you realize in less than a week Lily and I will be married? I just keep pinching myself. I'm one lucky guy."

"That you are, my boy. Doug, I have something to talk to you about."

"You sound so serious. Are you feeling all right?"

"Yes, I'm as fine as I can be with this controlling Parkinson's. That is part of what I want to talk about. You know that chances are that if I live long enough I will be disabled and maybe in a wheel chair. I won't be able to care for Sarah as I should. I would like to ask you if you would be her official guardian. Sarah and I have talked about this at length and we agree you're the one."

"Did you have any doubt I wouldn't say yes? I'll be honored to do that for you, Abe. I love Sarah as a mother and with Lily's help she will be cared for in the best possible way."

"Thank you, Doug. You're a good man even if you do throw fish back!"

"Are the plans for the wedding on schedule? I know the women have been buzzing for days."

"I believe everything is on schedule. Lily doesn't tell me when something goes wrong."

"That's usually good thinking." Abe chuckled to himself.

*****

Lily, awoke early. She quietly walked down the hall to Anna Rose's room. Peeking in to make certain she was still asleep, she was surprised to see her tip toeing around the room. She was carrying the little white basket she would use later today to hold the white rose petals.

"Look at the beautiful flower girl! This is the day, sweetheart! Do you have butterflies in your tummy, too?

Anna Rose looked down at her stomach with a puzzled look.

Lily laughed. Never mind. We have nothing to be nervous about. I've been married to this man before. Or have I really? He has certainly changed in many ways. Sometimes I hardly know him. Realizing the child did not understand, she smiled and said, "and he is your Daddy." Anna Rose clapped her hands with the basket swinging on her arm.

"Thank you, God," Lily whispered.

The house was quiet. She put her fingers to her lips and she and the toddler made their way to the kitchen.

Everyone would probably sleep for another hour. Lily thought of the many incidents of the past week. It began with the Will and Teresa's visit. It was difficult for her not to laugh when Teresa found out that there was only $500.00 in the account. She felt guilty that she had gloated but Teresa needed to learn that she has no people skills. Lily's feelings about Teresa were fluid; sometimes she liked her and sometimes she did not. The truth of the matter was that she didn't trust her. Something must have gone very wrong in her childhood.

Lily brought her thoughts back to her long list of things to do before her wedding. Number one, would Anna

Rose walk down the aisle with a basket of rose petals?" Would it be safer if someone like Sarah was nearby to handle little emergencies? Lily wanted her to be in the wedding and what did it matter if she strayed a little? I'll just quit worrying about it, she thought to herself.

As the wedding day drew closer, Doug, was getting butterflies, too. He cannot remember feeling this way the first time, but that was different. He and Lily eloped. There was just a tiny part of him that wished they had planned to do the same this time. Weddings and all their trappings seemed a waste of time and money. He knew he would never express this to Lily. She felt cheated the first go round with no wedding with family and friends. He wouldn't say this out loud. But this wedding was a gift from him.

Rose had dropped in for short visits more frequently. James Andrew was growing so fast. Anna Rose thought he was a doll and she kept pointing and saying: "She dress? Dress?" She had never seen a boy doll.

Sarah took charge of Anna Rose. With her training as a nanny she had her ways of getting children to do what they should do. Rose left her baby with a babysitter. He was just a little young to understand Momma's responsibilities at the wedding.

All the attendants were gathered upstairs at Bittersweet. James had given the whole house over to the wedding party. He stayed at the little cottage where Margaret and Rose lived before he and Margaret were married. He rather enjoyed the change and Margaret's memories seemed more vivid here. He could not put into words how her death had affected him. At first he

134

contemplated suicide but a little voice kept saying, "don't do it. Margaret will know." Slowly the thoughts went away. His understanding of heaven wasn't quite clear but he had faith that it would be good. He looked forward to meeting Margaret there.

****

"Is everybody ready to give your attention to Lily? After all she is the star of this party." Rose looked like a teenager in her pastel yellow dress of delicate lace. The lace was Margaret's idea. She had seen it in a woman's magazine and thought it would be beautiful. The other attendants wore dresses of mint green lace. They carried nosegays of yellow spring flowers and baby's breath. Lily carried white calla lilies. Anna Rose's dress was white lace trimmed in embroidered yellow flowers. She carried a white basket of white rose petals.

The organist struck the first chord of "Joyful, Joyful, We Adore Thee." and the procession began. It seemed that the congregation had been holding their breaths as if on cue, they all breathed out at once. The young women and one little girl were breathtaking. Aunt Margaret's presence was there in every lace dress.

Tears were softly falling into James' lap. There was sniffling throughout the little chapel. But there were two faces beaming with new found love.

The ceremony was over and the young couple turned to face the guests. Arm in arm they took their first steps as Mr. and Mrs. Douglas Lawson. Anna Rose followed close behind. The chapel was filled with family and friends, such a sea of faces.   As Rose passed the last pew, one face stood out.

"Oh, no it couldn't be him. She grabbed the end of the pew.